SORCHA MOWBRAY

# One Night With A Cowboy

*Books 1-5*

First published by Amour Press 2015

Cover art by Sorcha Mowbray. Images used from Period Images and Unsplash.com.

Second edition

This book was professionally typeset on Reedsy.
Find out more at reedsy.com

# Contents

# Taking Her Chance

*One Night with a Cowboy*
Book 1
By
Sorcha Mowbray

# Chapter One

Beth Torrence sat back in the aerodynamic Herman Miller task chair. It was one a.m. and her screen looked fuzzy around the edges. *Guess I should call it a night,* she thought. She reached up to switch her screen off, but an email notification popped up. It was from Soul Mates Dating service. Beth's gut clenched. Damn, she had just turned her paperwork in the day before.

Her hand shook, but she opened the email and read.

*Dear Ms. Torrence,*

*I am delighted to tell you that your date has been arranged for two days from now. You will arrive at the Golden Mustang Dude Ranch midmorning, settle in, and maybe go for a horseback ride if you so desire. Your date will join you in your room at sunset. Room service will be at your disposal or, if you prefer, you may go to the dining room to eat. Enjoy and remember to make the most of this chance.*

*Selena Markam*

*President and CEO*

*Soul Mates Dating*

"Deep breaths. I can do this." Beth shut her computer down and headed home to try and get some sleep. She set the alarm code for the office and walked out of Torrence Advertising. After busting her ass for six years building her business from nothing, she deserved this treat for herself. Soul Mates Dating was the most exclusive dating service around. If Beth hadn't had a client recommend it she would have ended up signing up for one of those cheesy dating sites online. Granted, she had filled in the paperwork at the urging of Sarah, her best friend, after they were halfway through the second bottle of wine on an epic girl's night; but deep down, she wanted this. It was time to see if she could date a man without comparing him to the one she had walked away from.

Chance Rogers could have been the best thing that ever happened to her, but she'd been too focused on her dream of becoming an advertising executive. The sparks that had flared between them and the sex that followed had scared the crap out of her because, for a brief moment, she could see herself settling down and forgetting her lifelong dream. She could see herself becoming her mother, who had given up everything only to be betrayed by a man who supposedly loved her.

History would not repeat itself, not with her.

Beth pulled into her parking spot and collected her things from the backseat. She'd brought some work home because she seriously doubted that she would be getting any sleep tonight. Between nerves about her date on Saturday and memories of Chance it was going to be a long night.

Chance pulled his truck into the long dirt drive of the dude ranch where he would meet his date. The email from Selena Markam, containing details of his date, had been a surprise after hearing nothing for nearly six months. Could his ideal date have been that hard to find? He wanted a woman who would be independent, sassy, but had room in her life and her heart for a broken-down old cowboy. His leg didn't hurt as bad as it had right after that last accident in the ring—I mean, who enjoyed being stepped on by 2 Tons of Fun? The upside had been that the bull only actually weighed a little over a ton—not two.

Tightening his sweaty palms on the steering wheel, he stopped at the main lobby and checked in. He was a bit early, but they had a room ready for him. He settled in and decided to take a shower to wash the grime of the road off. As usual, he couldn't help but think about the woman he would meet. Elizabeth was all he was given as a name. He wondered if she looked like the girl he requested. The memory of long dark hair and big blue eyes flashed across his mind. It still baffled him how one night of mind-blowing sex could stay with a man for almost ten years. How it could haunt him to the point that all other women came up short, including the jezebel he'd married.

Showered, shaved, and freshly dressed, he checked the printout of the email for the millionth time. It gave strict instructions that he should be at her door at sunset. She had one of the little cabins on the outer edges of the property, so it would take him a few minutes to walk over. Tamping down his nerves, which he was mildly distressed to realize were way worse than when he was about to pop out of the chute on 2,700 pounds of bull, he sauntered out of his room and headed toward his chance at a future. One, he hoped, without impossible expectations of some woman whom he had started to believe never existed.

The sun sat low in the sky, casting a deep orange glow over the dusty ranch. This was his favorite time of day back home. The day's work completed, what lay ahead included a good meal, a cold beer, and the satisfaction of another job well done. He found her door and knocked.

"Come on in," a muffled but feminine voice called through the door.

He took a deep breath and opened the door. Her back was to him, but instantly he could see she was everything he had asked for. Long dark hair hung loose around her shoulders and covered what appeared to be a red sleeveless shirt. A trim waist flared out to a curvaceous ass, which her denim skirt barely covered, that begged to have his hands on it. Her long legs seemed to go on forever despite the red cowgirl boots she wore. His breath rushed out as his cock leapt to attention. Mentally he begged her to turn around. If she had blue eyes he might leap on her straight away and skip the preliminaries.

"Hi there," was all he could come up with to say since every drop of blood in his body had departed his thinking head.

She turned around and it was like a physical blow to his solar plexus. He could only liken it to being stomped on by a bull. Elizabeth was Beth. The Beth of his dreams, the woman who got away.

"Chance?" She looked as stunned as he was by the unexpected turn of events.

# Chapter Two

Someone had sucked all the air out of the room because Beth was hallucinating. No way could Chance Rogers be standing in her cabin. "What are you doing here?"

He flinched at the harshness of her question. "I'm your date." A cautious, lopsided smile curved one side of his kissable lips as he plucked the Stetson from his head and dropped it on a nearby table.

"That can't be right." Confusion swirled through her, making her dizzy. "My date's name is Aaron." She walked, staggered really, over to her purse and pulled out a sheet of paper. "Yep. Right here it says Aaron will arrive at sunset."

"I'm Aaron." He walked toward her in slow, measured steps. The thud of his boots sounded loud in the quiet of the room. "I used my middle name because I didn't want anyone recognizing me."

"Who would recognize you?" Blown away by the fact that Chance stood before her, she couldn't really follow his train of thought.

"Fans, buckle bunnies, the media. This night was meant to be a private thing for me. Only my brother knows where I am." He shrugged and stepped into her personal space, crowding her and making it impossible to think.

"So, you're famous. For what?" A quick step backward gave her some breathing space.

"Bull riding. I hit it big on the PBR tour and picked up a ton of endorsement deals. I retired six months ago, but folks just don't seem to understand that I am not going to ride bulls again."

"Oh. I had no clue. Isn't that dangerous?" Fear gripped her gut at the notion he had put himself in danger.

"Yeah, but only when I wasn't on the bull." He flashed a megawatt smile that made her toes curl and her body overheat.

"Wow. So this is real. You're my date?" Her voice squeaked on the last word.

"It looks that way. Is that gonna be okay with you, or are you gonna cut and run again?" His hands fisted at his sides as he waited for her response.

For a moment, she really wasn't sure what her answer would be. Part of her wanted to flee in embarrassment for what had happened almost ten years earlier. The other part screamed for her to wrap her arms around him and never let him go. She drew a deep breath and allowed her gaze to meet with his. "I'm not going anywhere, cowboy."

His hands relaxed and he stepped in to her. Strong arms circled her waist and pulled her against his chest. The feel of Chance's lips on hers was a sensation she had long fantasized about, but reality far outstripped her memories. His firm, masculine lips settled over hers and pressed lightly at first. Soon his tongue dragged along the seam, seeking entrance to her mouth. She opened to him, growing dizzy from the lack of oxygen accompanied by a rush of warmth as he swept into her mouth to taste and caress. A low moan escaped from her and her knees turned to jelly. If his strong arms had not been supporting her, she would have puddled at his feet.

He groaned as he deepened the kiss, bending her near in half. Her hands settled on his wide shoulders, gripping him with a fierce intensity that mirrored their kiss. Hot flashes skipped across her skin as darts of pleasure zipped down to her pussy. Dear God, she wanted this man with an intensity to rival the sun. He pulled away from her, ending the kiss.

"Baby, I've been wanting to do that for damn near ten years." His eyes blazed desire as his gaze roved over her face and down her upper body. Their hips remained fused together, letting her feel the hard ridge of his cock.

"You aren't the only one that suffered all that time." She tried to give him a sultry smile, but regret washed through her with such a powerful force that she stepped away from him and broke their embrace.

"Why did you cut and run, Beth? I woke up alone and thought maybe I had imagined having the best sex of my life with the most amazing woman I'd ever met." The hurt in his voice only added fuel to the bonfire of her regrets.

Heat suffused her face, so she glanced at her watch to stall. "Maybe we should go have some dinner…"

Her sexy cowboy watched her carefully and apparently decided to cut her a little slack. "Okay. Dinner and talking first." He nodded and turned toward the door. Picking up his hat to plop it on his head, he glanced back over his shoulder. "You coming?"

She let out the breath she was holding and snatched up her purse. Pulling up alongside Chance, she smiled again and attempted to casually stroll out. Turned out it was more of a run. He closed the door behind them and reached out to grab her hand. "There's no race to win baby, let's walk slow and easy. Maybe watch the sun finish setting."

"Sorry." Her heart pounded in her chest.

They strolled at a leisurely pace toward the main building, neither saying a word. Beth continued to worry about all the things that plagued her before. Could she trust him? Would he expect her to cook and clean for him? She really wasn't the domestic type. What about her business? Could he live with a successful woman? Silently, she chewed her lip and worried all the way to dinner.

The maître d' sat them in a quiet corner of the restaurant that lent itself to cozy, intimate conversation. Seated, they looked over the menus. After a few minutes the waiter approached and took their order, which included a bottle of the merlot that Chance preferred when drinking wine.

Beth looked awful nervous sitting across the table. Once the wine was uncorked, tasted, and approved, the sommelier poured for the lady and then him. Alone again, he sipped the buttery red wine and watched the woman he'd dreamed of nervously guzzle hers. He leaned over and refilled her empty glass. Their salads came and after few more minutes of strained silence punctuated by chewing, he asked, "What have you been doing since college?"

She cleared her throat. "Working." She paused to glance around the room as though the answers were hidden in a corner. "I work in advertising. Started out as an account executive and now I run my own agency. It's taken six years, but Torrence Advertising is finally operating in the black and we're winning top clients from some of the bigger New York City firms."

While talking about her business she exuded a confidence that eradicated the nervousness. Her eyes sparkled and her voice grew strong with the conviction of what she was doing. Chance found it sexy as hell. "Advertising is a tough game. You must be fearsome in the boardroom."

"Well, fearsome is a bit strong. I certainly don't pull punches though. I play to win every time I pitch a new campaign. How about you? You said earlier that your rodeo days were over. Why?"

The waiter arrived with their meals, giving him a moment to prepare to answer her question. His accident wasn't something he talked about a whole lot. She cut into her steak and looked up at him expectantly. "I got my leg stepped on by a bull nearly a year and a half ago. The break took three months to heal and then another three months for me to be able to walk right. From there I tried for six months to get back in the ring, but my leg just doesn't feel the same. As much as I love bull riding, it just ain't worth getting killed over. Besides, with all my endorsement money and some investments I made, I don't actually need to rodeo anymore. Now I'm happy to work my ranch and manage my business interests."

"Well, I'm glad you were smart enough to stop when your body called it quits. What kind of business interests do you have?" She ate her steak with gusto, all trace of her nerves gone.

"Let's see, I have my clothing and riding tack lines along with a line of boots. I've also invested in some startup businesses that I'm waiting to see pan out."

"Holy cow, Chance. You really did hit it big in the PBR. I'm impressed you did something with your good fortune besides piss it away on beer and… what did you call them? Buckle bunnies?" She laughed a deep sultry chuckle that warmed his insides and made his cock stand up and take notice. That, along with the tantalizing vee of her neckline, and he could have skipped the rest of dinner to get straight to dessert.

"My mama always said idle hands did the devil's work. Besides, my body was my way of life for years before I hit it big. What good was wrecking that with booze, women, and late nights? I watched too many good cowboys wash out from playing hard in and out of the ring." He wiped his mouth with his napkin and set it aside. "So, Beth, are you going to explain to me why you ditched me that night? Because I'm not comfortable with this date going any further until I understand what happened." He reached across the table and rested his hand on top of hers.

She flushed red again, hesitated. With a big sigh, she raised her gaze to meet his and nodded. "I guess you deserve an answer. Before I was born, my mamma was an up-and-coming model. She had a contract with a big New York modeling agency and was planning to move there in a few weeks. Then she met my daddy at a Houston honky-tonk. It was love at first sight, she said. Two weeks later she bailed on her contract, married my daddy, and settled down to take care of him. Nine months after that, I showed up and then in another two years came my little sister." She took a sip of her wine, and when she looked back at him her eyes were filled with sadness.

"What happened, baby?" He squeezed the hand he still held captive.

"My mamma took us and we went to visit grandma, but we came home a day early. We walked in on my daddy chasing some naked twenty-year-old blonde around the house. Me just a toddler and my sister still in diapers, poor mamma took us and fled the house. She drove us around for hours before she could walk back in that house. When she did, he was gone. He left a note and said he'd made a mistake marrying her. A few weeks later the divorce papers came. It turned out he'd been cheating on her the entire time they were married. She was left destitute. No money. No job. No skills. She sold the house, moved home with her mamma, and worked as a waitress at a diner until I could afford to take care of her.

"Anyway, fast forward to the night we met. From my point of view, it could only be classified as magical. It was everything mamma said love could be, and it scared the ever-loving hell out of me. Pictures of us living in domestic bliss flashed through my head, but not one of those pictures included me putting on a suit and going to work at an advertising agency. The fear of making the same mistake my mamma did drove me out of your bed and kept

9

me from returning your phone calls."

"Oh, baby, I wasn't looking for a wife back then. Nor have I ever wanted to keep a woman barefoot and pregnant in my kitchen. Your drive to succeed was, and still is, one of the most attractive things about you." His heart ached for everything they'd missed out on because she hadn't stuck around to talk about her fears.

"I'm so sorry I didn't give you a chance. I just knew if you opened your mouth and tried to sweet-talk me into giving up everything I wouldn't have been able to say no. I needed to experience success in my own right. I've paid the price for that choice every night and day since then." She picked up their joined hands and rubbed her cheek against his knuckles.

He groaned, wanting desperately to be in her room, alone and naked.

"No man has measured up to my memory of you. It didn't take me long to quit trying to date. Work became my sole focus and it paid off in that I have my own agency. But there's still a big, huge gaping hole in my life."

Chance felt his mouth go dry as the Chihuahuan Desert. He'd heard enough; it was time to pick up where they'd left off all those years ago. "Come on, baby. I think I've got just the thing to start filling that hole." He stood up, pulled her chair out for her, and slung a possessive arm around her shoulders. She belonged to him and he wanted every man on the Golden Mustang Dude Ranch to know it. Hell, he wanted every man within a one-hundred-mile radius to know it.

# Chapter Three

Beth opened the door to her cabin and gasped. On every available surface candles were strewn, casting a soft glow on the big open room.

He leaned over and whispered into her ear. "Do you like it, baby?"

"Oh, Chance, it's amazing. When did you have this done?"

Taking off his Stetson, he slipped past her, set it on a chair, and pulled the champagne out of the ice bucket. "I had a signal set up with the waiter. When I ordered the wine he knew to get the wheels in motion and set this up." He popped the cork and poured two glasses of effervescent wine. He glanced at her, unsure for a moment. "I wasn't sure who I was going to meet here tonight and well, if we hadn't clicked I wouldn't have wanted to put any pressure on you or whoever else it might have been. But if there was a spark, I wanted to be prepared. I just could never have guessed that I would have walked in to find you."

"I still can't believe it. I mean I submitted my application just a few days ago." She shook her head and then sipped the straw-colored liquid.

"A few days! I've been waiting for six months." Chance sounded almost disgruntled.

Laughter bubbled up from deep within. "Let me guess, you basically described me on your application? Because I absolutely requested an exact replica of you, at least what I could remember."

He laughed. "Yeah, I did the same thing. I wonder how Selena Markam knew to wait? How she knew you would eventually seek out her services?"

"I don't know, but honestly at this moment I'm not looking a gift horse in

11

the mouth."

"I agree." He set his glass down and stalked toward her like a mountain lion hunting a deer. Cornering her against the bed, he pulled her flute from her suddenly nerveless fingers. "I want to taste your sweet lips again, Beth."

A dull throbbing pulsed between her legs that matched the racing rhythm of her heart. Earlier she'd been so stunned at seeing him that their kiss floated like a light haze over her memory. His hands landed on her hips and pulled her in close. She slipped her tongue out to moisten her parched lips and slid her arms up around his neck. He stared directly into her eyes, leaving no question what he wanted from her. His tongue surged into her mouth, staking his claim. The dampness between her legs seeped into her lacy panties and her nipples hardened.

He touched, stroked, and tasted every crevice of her mouth in the most erotic kiss she had ever been party to. Had he gotten better at kissing? She would have sworn there was nothing to improve on before, but this... This assault could only be described as mind-blowing. Desperate for more, she pressed herself closer to him. His arms tightened around her and then they were falling.

With a little grunt from him, they landed on the bed and rolled so that his body pinned her beneath him. He broke the kiss and smiled down at her. "Now I've got you right where I want you."

She giggled and pressed a kiss to his jaw, followed by another, and another. Craving the feel of his skin against hers, she began tugging his shirt out of his pants. "Shirt. Off."

"Yes, ma'am." He lifted up and knelt, straddling her hips. In short order his shirt disappeared, revealing a toned and sexy chest that cried out for her attention. Beth couldn't help but lick her lips in anticipation of kissing every inch of his skin.

Before she could put into action her very lusty thoughts, he had the hem of her shirt in his hands, tugging it off. His eyes lit up when he spied her black lace bra. Warm masculine hands gently cupped her breasts on top of the lace and he flicked his thumbs over the distended nipples. Her breath caught in her throat, pleasure shooting from her puckered nubs to her pussy.

"I take it you have matching panties under that nothing of a skirt?" His voice sounded strained, almost a growl.

"Mmmm. I know one way you can find out." Did she just purr at him? Something about this man made her feel ultra-sexy.

"So do I." He slid off and stood her up at the side of the bed. With the flick of a wrist her skirt gapped open and slid down her legs. She stood before him in nothing but black lace and a pair of red cowgirl boots. "Dear Lord, give me strength," he mumbled before suckling one lace-covered breast. Switching to the other side, he cupped her ass and kneaded. All the while, Beth fought the urge to shove him back and cover his torso with kisses. In the end she lost the battle.

With a little cry of frustration, she pushed him back on the bed and clambered over him. With his hips pinned securely under her, she ran her fingers over the flat, disk-like nipples that peeked out from under a light dusting of hair. "Sorry, I couldn't wait my turn." She waggled her eyebrows and bent over to trace the path her fingers took with her tongue.

"By all means." He groaned and gripped her hips as she teased his nipples. His big hands slid around and gripped her ass, grinding her against his trapped erection. She moaned and swirled her hips. Moving down his torso, she found the impediment of his belt buckle. Dipping her tongue into his belly button, she worked the buckle loose and then opened his jeans.

Oh glory be! The man went commando. Eager now to fully unwrap her present, she yanked his pants down his legs and discovered that he still had his boots on. Double damn. For the moment she would work around it. Turning back to his exposed cock she licked her lips in anticipation. He was beautifully made—long enough to give her pause and thick enough that her fingers just missed connecting. And best of all, he was hers, at least for tonight.

She paused but pushed away the unwanted thought that maybe this could be a second chance at a future. For now she wanted a second chance at tasting the man himself. Leaning over, she slid her tongue over the head of his cock and dipped into the slit that leaked a drop of pre-come. The slight saltiness of the clear fluid teased her tongue and made her hungry for more.

13

Relaxing her throat and mouth, she sank down on his hard shaft, swallowing him whole. It was more than she'd ever taken like this, and she had to focus to let him slip into the back of her throat. But heaven help her, it was worth it to watch his eyes widen in shock and feel his hands thrust into her hair.

"Oh, baby. Yes," he muttered, followed by a deep, chest-rumbling groan.

She lifted up and then repeated the process, sinking back down.

"Do you know how gorgeous you are? Damn, woman." His hips thrust forward, meeting her downward stroke. "So sexy watching you take me like this after imagining it so many nights."

She matched the rhythm he set, reveling in the taste of him and the sheer power she held in pleasuring him like this. After a few more strokes he pushed her away.

"So good, baby, but I want to come inside you with your sweet heat wrapped around my cock."

Her pussy clenched in response to his words as her juices flooded her panties. She wanted that too. "Oh, Chance. Yes. Please. Now."

"Soon. First I want to taste your sweet honey. Help me take my boots off."

She climbed off the bed and straddled one leg with her ass facing him. She bent over and tugged on the boot. She had it halfway off when his finger slid up her aching slit and swirled around her entrance. "Oh, Chance." She pushed back onto his finger, enjoying the delicious slide of his thick digit into her hot sheath.

"My boot, baby." He withdrew his finger.

Looking over her shoulder, she shot him a nasty glare. Stupid man. Pulling the boot free, she switched legs and removed the other one before he could tease her further. Boots gone, she finished off his pants and socks, leaving him as naked as the day he was born.

Sitting down, she took care of her own boots, but before she could strip the black lace away, he stopped her.

"Hold on. I want to take care of all the lacy parts." His wicked smile promised she would enjoy letting him have his way. He started by nibbling on her lips. His molten kisses soon trailed down her jaw to her neck and over her collarbones. Each touch of his mouth on her skin sent ripples of pleasure coursing through her body. Finally he reached behind her and unhooked her bra, letting it slide forward to unveil her breasts.

"Baby, those may be the prettiest titties I have ever seen." He reminded himself not to pounce on the poor woman. Though at the moment, she looked as though she might welcome a little pouncing. He pressed her back onto the bed and straddled her hips so that he could feast on her pink-tipped breasts.

He could easily spend the next twenty or thirty years enjoying those luscious mounds and not get tired of doing so. The soft flesh molded to his big hands, and every stroke or touch seemed to cause her to shiver. Sucking in earnest, he loved that she knotted her fingers in his hair as though she might not ever let him stop.

Bound and determined to move south, he had to tug a bit to get her to let go. Sliding down, he knelt on the floor and spread her legs. With a smooth pull of her hips, he slid her ass to the edge of the bed and managed to pull her thong down and then off. He spread her legs wide and drove his tongue deep into her sopping entrance. Something primal clawed its way up from the depths of his soul and claimed her. Then and there it screamed out mine. She was his and no other would touch her again. Ever.

He plunged his tongue in and out, mimicking what he wanted to do with his cock. Her needy core clenched around him, trying to keep him with her. He slid two fingers deep into her heat as he switched to flicking the turgid little peak with his tongue. She moaned and thrust her hips against his mouth and hand.

"Please. Chance, I need more. I need you to be inside me." Her husky pleadings grated on his tenuous control.

"Soon, baby. I promise; first I want you to come for me. Can you do that? Can you come for me?" He resumed working her clit with his tongue as he thrust his fingers deep into her pussy.

Her body tensed and she gripped his head. "Yes!"

"That's it, baby, yell for me. Nobody can hear you but me." Her cries, paired with the rapid thrust of her hips, told him in no uncertain terms that she was about to explode. And then she did. The walls of her sheath clamped down on his fingers as her juices flooded his hand. He kept stroking her clit, letting her cries ring through the room. After pulling his fingers from her, he proceeded to lick them clean. Her eyes tracked the flicks of his tongue as he lapped up every bit of her delicious offering.

Reaching to the floor for his jeans, he produced a little foil packet. Sheathing himself in the rubber, he spread her legs and pressed the tip of his throbbing cock to her entrance. He stopped. "Beth, baby. Look at me." He waited until her gaze locked with his. "I won't let you go again." He pushed forward and buried himself deep in her body. His balls nestled up against her ass, surrounding him in her heat. Being inside a woman never felt so good.

Dragging backwards out of her body, he stopped short of full withdrawal, only to drive back in. He pistoned in and out of her, pushing them both toward the release only orgasm could bring. Her walls clenched and rippled around him while he strummed her clit with his thumb.

"Yes, Chance. Yours. I'm yours." Her words shot clear to his heart and crumbled what little remained of his defenses.

As she shattered around him, it was all he could do to stop himself from declaring his newfound feelings. It was too soon to say it, but the emotions were real. His balls tightened just before ecstasy took over. His release shimmied down his spine and curled his toes. Sliding from her warmth, he tossed the condom and settled them under the covers.

"Baby, I meant what I said. This doesn't end tonight." He spooned her from behind, settling one hand on her breast. Lazily he stroked the nipple, enjoying the feel of her skin against his.

"I'm glad. I want to see where this leads. I can't imagine walking away for a second time."

"Good. Now get some rest; you're gonna need it." He kissed the top of her head and snuggled down.

Morning came bright and early after being up half the night making love with Chance. Beth rolled over and smiled. Somehow fate had intervened and given her another chance at love.

His lashes lifted and a grin split his face. "Morning, baby."

"Morning, cowboy. Are you hungry for some breakfast? We could order room service." She sat up and stretched, but was quickly pulled back into the bed and tucked against him.

"In a minute. First I need my good-morning kiss." He pressed his lips to hers, sweeping into her mouth with his tongue. She moaned and melted against him. Pulling back to peck her lips a few more times, he released her. "Now, let me see to ordering us some breakfast." He got out of bed and handed her a menu. "Tell me what you'd like."

She scanned the menu. "Two eggs scrambled, bacon, and pancakes. I seem to have worked up an appetite."

Chance called and placed their order. "In the meantime, we need to talk." His heart raced as he watched some of the tension from yesterday ease into her features.

"Okay. What's on your mind, cowboy?" Her nonchalance rang false and grated on his good mood.

"Don't do that. Don't ever hide your emotions behind a façade. I'll always want to know what you're thinking and feeling."

Her eyes widened in surprise, but she nodded. "I'm sorry. You're right, that was rude of me. I can't expect you to be honest with me if I won't be honest with you."

"It's okay, baby. I just don't want any barriers between us. If we're going to be together, we have to be open to each other. No holding back. I want you to move in with me at my ranch. It's about forty minutes outside of Houston, so you could go in to the office when you need to and I can give you an office to work from at my place." He held his breath as he waited for her response.

"Oh. I wasn't expecting that. I thought we'd date and see where this goes."

"Maybe I'm just being greedy, but I want to go to sleep with you in my arms at night and wake up that way in the morning. I want to watch you brush your teeth while I shave, see your socks and panties in the drawer next to my shorts, and I want to eat every meal with you across the table. I told you last night I wasn't ever letting you go, and I meant it." He reached out to trace the line of her jaw.

She said nothing for a few moments, and he watched the myriad emotions flicker across her face. Finally, something won out, but he wasn't sure what. "I want that too, but I'm not ready to jump in blind. I'll move in with you, but I'm keeping my place for a while. Just until we're both sure this arrangement will work. Can you live with that?"

"Yeah. I don't like it, but I can live with it. For now. Don't think I won't be working hard to convince you to make it a more permanent arrangement." He resisted the urge to pout. Apparently the hardheaded woman didn't realize that what they had was special. But he'd show her once he got her home. If he had to tie her to the bed, he'd make her see that she wasn't going anywhere.

"I look forward to being persuaded." A sultry grin curved her lips up.

"Well then, I should get started right away." He pulled her into his arms and kissed her like he'd never let her go—mostly because he wouldn't.

# Epilogue

Beth rose from her desk and wandered through the house she shared with Chance. Everything in her wanted to latch on to the man she loved and never let go. But despite the idyllic six months they'd lived together since their one-night stand, she hadn't truly been able to commit. She was beginning to suspect that she could only do it if she let her apartment go. Though she had yet to say the words, she knew she loved him with all her heart. It terrified her that because of that love she was so vulnerable.

As for Chance, he'd been nothing but patient, wooing her over romantic dinners and with creatively erotic lovemaking. It seemed he'd left no stone unturned in his campaign to prove to her they belonged together. All except saying the words. Neither of them had strung those three most-important words together. She'd been as remiss as he in not being honest about her feelings. It was time to correct that oversight. Taking a deep breath, she stepped out of the house, determined to go find her man and stake her claim for the final time.

It was time to take her Chance.

The sun sat low in the afternoon sky, even as the heat of the day still simmered in the air. She plucked at her tank top and headed toward the barn. Inside, she found Chance bare-chested, spreading fresh hay in the stalls. Licking her lips, she resisted the urge to pinch herself. He belonged to her, and she to him. Now she needed to make sure that it would be a permanent arrangement.

"Hey there, cowboy." Her voice came out thick and husky with desire.

He stopped and turned around. His smile alone sent moisture pooling between her thighs and made her knees weak. "Hey there, baby. How's your day going?"

"It's getting better and better," she said and walked toward him.

"How so?" His eyebrow quirked up in question.

"Mmmm… Well, I was lucky enough to stumble upon a half-naked cowboy who looks like he could use a rub-down." She pulled up in front of him and rubbed his rapidly hardening cock.

"Rubbing sounds good. But let me go clean up first." He stepped back.

"I don't think I want to wait. Beside, you smell good. Like sweat and man." She flicked her tongue out and slicked it up his damp pectoral.

He groaned. "Woman, what has got into you?"

"Hopefully you." She tangled her arms around his neck.

"You are playing with fire, baby. Are you prepared to get burned?" His voice sounded as though it croaked out of a throat as dry as dust.

"As long as you put out the flames." She pulled his head down so she could plant her lips on his and proceeded to lay claim to him. Sliding her tongue inside, she tangled with his, battling for control.

Breaking the kiss, he pulled back. "Oh, baby, you've no idea what you started. But I'm gonna show you."

"Please, Chance." Her whimpered words were all she could manage after that blazing hot kiss.

"Strip. I want you naked. Now." He stepped back from her and stripped his work gloves off. Leaning against a saddle stand covered with only a blanket, he watched.

She reached for her red boot.

"Leave the boots. I like you wearing nothing but those sexy red cowgirl boots. Besides, it's safer in here to keep them on."

She nodded, pulled her tank over her head, and dropped it on a nearby hay bale. Reaching behind her, she unhooked her bra and tossed it with her shirt. Then she unfastened her shorts and pushed them down her thighs along with her panties. Naked but for her boots, her heart raced in anticipation of what Chance would do.

His cock strained against the fly of his jeans, but he made no move to remove them. He raised his hand and curled his finger toward himself. "Come here, baby."

She took the few steps needed to cover the distance between them, and he pulled her into his arms. Fisting his hands in her hair, he savaged her mouth in a fierce kiss that commanded and demanded as it took. She was lost, burning up with need for him. There wasn't enough water in the stock tank to douse the fire raging through her.

The kiss deepened, devastating her ability to think. That was probably why she didn't realize what he'd done until it was too late. He broke the kiss and put his hands on her shoulders to steady her as they straightened. "Chance?"

"Do you trust me, baby?" His gaze locked with hers and he looked so vulnerable, as vulnerable as she felt with her hands tied behind her back.

Did she trust him? The answer that screamed back at her was a resounding yes. He would never hurt her. In that instant she felt all her walls drop, and she knew she would tell him exactly what she had come out here to say. "Yes. I trust you, cowboy. I love you too much not to."

He gasped. Seemed to stand unnaturally still and then he hauled her in for another kiss. Taking her mouth, he tasted her, stroked and nibbled until he was peppering kisses along her jaw and down toward her breasts. "Oh God, baby, I've been waiting months to hear you say those words. I love you so much I thought I'd go mad trying to prove it to you without scaring you half to death."

"I'm sorry I waited so long to say it," she replied, and then his mouth engulfed her erect nipple and all thought was lost again.

He suckled her nipples, rasping them with his tongue and nipping with his teeth. Hands bound behind her back with a tack rope, all she could do was feel. Her senses were on overload as he made love to her breasts. She moaned in pleasure and in need. "Please, Chance. Touch me."

"Aww, baby, I am touching you." He continued his sensual torture.

"My pussy. Please, between my legs." The ache was so intense she was sure it would turn into physical pain soon.

Pulling away, he turned them around and bent her over the saddle stand so that her belly lay across the blanket covering the wood arch that normally held a saddle. She couldn't see anything but the side of the stand. Then his feet nudged hers apart until she had a wide stance that left her open and fully exposed.

"Baby, if you want to stop at any point just say the word 'dog' and I'll know you really need me to stop. Okay?"

"Okay." Excitement rolled through her like a stampede.

"Your pussy is so pretty I can't get enough of looking at it. And you taste so sweet. You're mine, Elizabeth Torrence, and I'll never give you up." His warm breath wafted against her already heated flesh, causing her to squirm. Then his tongue slid from the front of her slit to her entrance and back. Her moan echoed through the barn and seemed to egg him on. He plunged a finger deep into her wet core and pumped it in and out as he licked her clit, just as he had done her nipples.

As she exploded around the single digit, he pulled it out and slid it into her anal passage. The sensual invasion seemed to fire off a second orgasm as he continued to work her pussy with his mouth, lapping at her juices. A second finger joined the first and worked in and out of her hole, using her own juices for lubrication. He'd done this before while buried deep inside her pussy, but this time he spread his fingers and stretched her more. She moaned as the pain of being stretched gave way to the pleasure his fingers brought, sliding in and out with a delicious friction. As he added a third finger, his tongue still drilling into her, another orgasm ripped through her. "Yes, Chance! Yes! Oh please, don't stop." Her cries mingled with his groans even as the powerful sensations ebbed. She heard him rise up behind her and walk away.

He came back and his boots stopped in front of her. The rasp of his zipper dropping was music to her ears. Gently he reached down and lifted her face up. "Suck me, baby. Suck my cock."

Hungry for any taste of him she could get, she took his head in her mouth and let him push forward. He slid deep until his balls bumped her chin and then drew back. Again he plunged into her mouth and retreated until he set up a maddening pace that left her body wanting more. Without warning, he pulled out and stepped away. His breath came in panting gasps, the only sound in the barn. She let her head drop back down and waited to see what was next.

Her arms ached from being behind her back for so long, but she wouldn't change a thing. She refused to say dog. This was everything she had ever wanted but could never have expressed. Her darkest fantasy pulled from her mind and brought to life by her very own sexy cowboy. Legs still spread, she felt a coolness land between the cheeks of her ass. "Chance, honey, what's that?"

"Lube, baby, to ease my way." He rubbed his cock through the folds of her pussy. "Are you okay?"

"Yes, but where did you get the lube? How did you know I was coming out here?" If she didn't focus on something other than the feel of his cock stroking her heated flesh, she would go insane.

"We keep some in the first aid kit for the horses. Now hush and just feel." He plowed into her pussy, driving his cock deep inside. His fingers pushed back in her backside and matched the rhythm he set with his shaft. Unable to do more than press her hips back to meet his thrusts, she was at his mercy. His wondrous and masterful mercy.

Then everything stopped. He pulled out of her sheath and removed his fingers. He placed the head of his cock at her tight rear pucker and pressed against the ring of muscle. Pressing back against him, she grew dizzy from the sensations spiraling through her. He pushed deep into her ass and seated himself to the hilt. "Oh, baby. You're so tight, so fucking tight. Can I move? Are you okay if I move?"

Her pussy clenched, making his cock feel thicker, longer, in her bottom. So good. "Fuck me, Chance. Please."

And he did. He pulled out and slid back in, pounding into her backside. The hard length of him filled her, stretched her, and gave her more pleasure than she had ever known. How she could have ever imagined that she didn't love him was impossible to fathom. All thought fled as she exploded in an earth-shattering orgasm that clenched his dick as he continued to pump into her. Then he came, shooting his load deep in her ass as he cried out, "I love you, Beth. Love you so damn much!" and collapsed over her.

A few moments later he lifted off her and slid out. He untied her hands and helped her stand up while he massaged her arms and fingers. "You okay, baby? I didn't hurt you, did I?"

"No, Chance, I loved every minute of what you did to me." She smiled and snuggled into his arms. "And I love you, cowboy."

"I love you too, baby." He clutched her close.

"Chance." Her voice wavered.

"Yeah?" He stilled.

"I'm ready to clear out my apartment."

"Oh, baby. Are you sure?" His hands cupped her face and his gaze locked with hers.

She nodded. "I've never been more sure of anything. I never want to let you go. You're mine, and I'm taking my Chance."

# Claiming His Cowgirl

*One Night with a Cowboy*
Book 2
By
Sorcha Mowbray

# Chapter One

Cassie bent over and jammed the shovel into the smelly mix of hay and horse dung. The pungent odor hung heavy in the air as she flung the shovelful of mixture into the wheelbarrow. Almost done. The streaming rays of sun licked the barn through the open door. Ownership of the Golden Mustang Dude Ranch was everything she'd dreamed of and more, with one small exception. Her ex-fiancé had ridden off into the sunset—without the girl. He'd lasted two months before declaring he couldn't handle ranch life.

Cassie snorted. Ranch life.

The dude ranch was so far removed from real ranch life it wasn't worth the effort to explain. The Mustang made good money from the guests that came for the atmosphere. Very few vacationers sought out a real ranch experience. They came to use the spa and lounge by the pool. In winter they came for the snow and the pageantry of Christmas. Most folks weren't looking for anything more ranch-like than a short jaunt on horseback.

If this were a real ranch, the animals they cared for would be their life's blood instead of relegated to ambiance. The last of the dirty hay landed in the wheelbarrow. Cassie wiped the sweat off her brow and set down the shovel. With a solid grip, she lifted the barrow and headed toward the compost pile. Hay and horseshit mixed with kitchen scraps made fantastic dirt. Back in the barn, she spread fresh hay in all the stalls she'd cleaned. The raspy rumble of a masculine throat clearing startled her.

"Shit! Do you always sneak up on people like that?" She returned to spreading hay.

"Sorry, ma'am." He tipped his hat in a mingled greeting-apology.

"No worries. I was probably over-focused on a simple task." She glanced back and smiled at him. Whoa. That was a real cowboy. Not some duded-up city boy. Worn jeans molded to strong thighs. His shirt fit him like it was made for him, and the Stetson on his head would have looked wrong anyplace else. She stopped spreading hay and faced the stranger. "Is there something I can do for you?"

"I was hoping to get in a quick ride. Feeling kind of antsy." He let his gaze drift down her body in a slow, blatant appraisal.

Her face heated, and it had nothing to do with her exertions. "The horses are in the corral. Everything you'll need is over there in the tack room." She pointed over her left shoulder.

"Thank ya kindly." The sexy cowboy smiled and sauntered past her.

What color were his eyes? She cursed the stupid hat for hiding the answer in the shadows.

Cassie pushed the sexy stranger from her mind and finished off her chores. Things were pretty quiet at the resort right now, so he must be one of a few daters they had as guests. About six months ago Soul Mates Dating Service contacted her about using her ranch. It seemed like a great source of supplemental income during the week. The ranch did a steady business, but it was a lot of weekend escapists from Houston rather than week-long vacationers, so the dating guests were a welcome addition during the week.

On her way back to the main lodge, Cassie spied the sexy man galloping across the field past the corral. He was riding Dark Knight, one of the stallions. He was a feisty ride, but the man looked as though he had everything under control.

A few hours and a quick shower later, she changed into some clean jeans, a pretty Western shirt, and her favorite boots. She decided to make a quick stop by the registration desk to check on things with the night manager.

"Hi, Ted. How are things tonight?" She shook his hand.

"Good. Most everyone has checked in." He smiled.

"Most everyone? Is someone missing?"

"Not missing. They called and cancelled at the last minute. It was one of the Soul Mates guests, a Miss Richards." He pointed to her name and info on the screen.

"All right. Did you let her date know of her cancellation?"

"Not yet. I was waiting on Julio to arrive so I might locate the gentleman. He wasn't in his room when I tried to phone him."

"Give me his name. I'll go track the poor man down." She grimaced, not relishing having to tell some guy he'd been stood up. She hoped to break it to him easy since she'd been on the receiving end of that information on more than one occasion.

"Trent Jones. You should find him in the bar, as that is where they were supposed to meet"—he glanced at his watch—"right now."

"Great. Any clue what he looks like?"

"Nope. I believe the instructions for the lady said he would be wearing a blue shirt and a black cowboy hat." Ted scrolled through the account notes. "Yep. Got it right here as backup info for her."

"All right. I better go break the news." Cassie shuffled off toward the bar. She stopped inside the entrance and scanned the room. There were a few couples that seemed to be engaged and a party of five men in the far corner. A lone man wearing the requisite blue shirt and black hat sat at the bar in direct sight of the door. He'd be hard to miss.

She sucked up her nerve and approached him. He turned when she was a few feet away. Her breath caught in an audible gasp that he no doubt caught. It was the sexy cowboy from earlier. What woman in her right mind would pass up a chance to meet this man? Cassie's mouth dried out, making speech impossible. The pleased grin on his sensual lips made her knees weak, resulting in her tripping on the carpet runner. As luck would have it, she landed in his arms.

A low chuckle skated over her skin, heightening her awareness as her nipples tightened and her hands squeezed his biceps. His hands rested on her hips with a firm grip that had her wanting to crawl into his lap. She steeled herself and stepped back.

Trent couldn't believe his luck. The sexy cowgirl from earlier was his date. He'd've sworn she worked there, but maybe they weren't mutually exclusive.

He took in her fiery red locks and the crisp apple green of her eyes. She was a beauty. He'd gotten so hard while he watched her lay fresh hay, imagined pulling her down to roll in it, that it took a while before he'd been able to straddle a horse without risking bodily harm.

Her pale, creamy complexion pinkened to a bright magenta that clashed adorably with her hair. She chewed her lower lip in apparent indecision and cleared her throat. "Uh, Mr. Jones I assume?"

"Yes. And you're Miss Richards?" There was no containing his grin.

"No. I'm afraid I'm not." She paused to take a breath, causing her breasts to thrust against her blouse in an enticing display. Disappointment rankled as he waited for her to continue. "See, the thing is Miss Richards cancelled her reservation a short while ago. She won't be meeting you."

"Well that's not all bad news." He savored the desire this woman stirred up.

"It's not?" Her brow wrinkled in consternation.

"Not a bit. If she's not here, that means I'm free to discover your name."

"Me?"

She seemed confused by his interest. "Yes, ma'am. You've had me hard as a fence post twice in the last few hours, and I don't even know your name. Now I can find it out and maybe coax you into eating dinner with me."

She flushed even brighter pink, not that he would have thought that possible. "I...I... No." She shook her head and took another step back. "I can't fraternize with the guests. Company policy."

Her stammering and stuttering was cute. "Oh, darlin', you can't possibly say no to the man you just dumped on behalf of some skittish woman," he cajoled with a smile.

She stood a bit straighter, and firming up her resolve, she replied, "I'm sorry, Mr. Trent, but the answer is no."

"Look, you've gotta eat right? Sit at a table with me so I don't have to feel awkward as I sit all alone." The strong-willed woman frustrated him. There was no way he would let her go without a name and dinner. "A simple dinner. Nothing more."

She eyed him, wariness causing her face to pinch and her eyes to narrow in speculation. "Fine. Dinner. But, keep in mind I've agreed because I wouldn't want to send a guest home dissatisfied."

*Now that sounds promising.* "Excellent. Are you ready, or is there something you need to take care of first?"

"I'm ready. I was headed in there anyway."

Her admission tickled him. "One more thing."

"What's that?" She twisted her hands.

# Chapter Two

"Why, your name. You still haven't told me your name, darlin'."

Her face blanked before she smiled as though laughing at herself. "Cassie. Cassie Truhart."

She stuck out her hand for a shake, but instead he grabbed it and hauled her up against his chest. "Darlin', we're far past a mere handshake. After all, you've dumped me."

He let her go in short order, but not far. He grabbed her hand again and led her toward the dining room.

"Good evening, Ms. Truhart. Dinner for... two?" The maître d' let his gaze zip back and forth between them.

"Yes, sir." Trent took control. "Reservation's under Jones, Trent Jones." He squeezed her hand, hoping to reassure her everything would be okay.

How did he get so damn lucky? He'd signed up for Soul Mates at the insistence of his perpetually meddling little sister, Sarah. Stubborn, she'd insisted after the bad breakup with his fiancée, spurred on by his discovering that not only had she lied about her pregnancy, but she had cheated on him with one of his ranch hands. He'd gone along with Sarah's idea because he didn't know how else to go about meeting women. Where he lived they were few and far between, and he'd never been a fan of the random bar pickup method.

He pulled the chair out for Cassie and seated himself next to her. No point in letting her out of his reach. Alone again, he took a moment to study her as she looked at the menu. "Thank you for joining me, Cassie. I didn't relish sitting here alone or holing up in my room for that matter."

"You're welcome. Like you said, a girl's gotta eat." She smiled.

"Well, you've eaten here before, what'd'ya recommend?"

"The steak is very good." Her impish smile caused his groin to tighten further.

"Imagine that. Guess I'll have the steak."

"It's quite good, but so is everything on the menu. I stole the chef from a four-diamond restaurant in Houston last year. I got lucky—he's a country boy at heart."

Trent stopped to process what she'd said. "So, if you work in personnel, what were you doing mucking out stalls?"

The waiter chose that moment to appear. They quickly placed their orders and were once again alone. Or mostly alone.

"What exactly do you do here at the Golden Mustang?" He rephrased his question, curious about the woman next to him.

"A little of everything. As the owner, no job is too big or too small."

Her statement left him reeling. She owned the damn place? The waiter arrived with their drinks and some bread before he melted away.

Trent grabbed his beer and took a quick swig to wet his whistle. "So you're telling me you own this whole spread?"

"I am." The words were a soft whisper as though she were embarrassed by the truth.

"Don't you have staff to take care of the stalls?" Most ranchers worked their own land, maybe hired help if their spread was big enough. But why would a resort owner need to do that kind of backbreaking labor?

"Sure, but I was born and raised in the country. I like mucking out the stalls and taking care of the horses. It's a nice break from paperwork and personnel." She laughed, a low smoky sound.

"I imagine it is, if that's what you like."

Good lord, the man was smoking hot and all but melted her panties when he smiled. His dark brown hair and big brown eyes sucked her in until she damn near forgot what they were talking about. "So, cowboy. What do you do? No wait, lemme guess." She paused, looked him up and down, and took a sip of her beer. "You're awful pretty, but not fancy enough to be on the pro-rodeo circuit."

He chuckled.

"I'd say you're a gentleman rancher. Cattle, not sheep." She nodded, confident in her assessment.

"You'd be spot on. I keep an average of six hundred head of cattle with enough land to accommodate all that entails."

Cassie whistled. "That sounds like some spread."

"I do all right. The land's been in the family for four generations. Now I run it for me and my baby sister. One day when she marries, her husband will take care of her part of the operation or I'll buy her out. In the meantime, I manage with some trusted hired hands whose families have worked our land for years."

"So what brought you to my resort? Why a dating service? A fine-looking man like you shouldn't have any problems with women." She was dying to know. It seemed ridiculous that he would need a matchmaking service.

"That can be laid at my baby sister's door. I went through a nasty breakup, ended an engagement last year. She thought this would be good for me, or at least better than picking up women down at the Busting Bronc, the local honky-tonk."

"Bad breakup? I'm just past my own failed attempt to get married." A certain kinship with the handsome man next to her wound its way through her soul.

"I can't imagine anyone leaving a woman like you." He snorted in disbelief.

"Well, this one did, couldn't cut it here. I didn't have the heart to tell him this wasn't real ranch life."

Trent guffawed and slapped his hand on his thigh. "Got yourself tied up with a city boy, huh?"

"Yeah. He thought he was a cowboy because he wore a hat and boots, but when the horse hit the trail, he bailed out of the saddle. What ended your attempt at marriage?"

"She was a liar and a cheater. Told me she was pregnant to get me to marry her, then proceeded to fuck one of my guys. I was so damn relieved when I learned the truth. I tossed her out without a lick of guilt."

"Sounds like you escaped by the skin of your teeth." Cassie decided then and there that she could spend all night listening to the bass rumble of his voice. Whether he was talking or laughing, his deep tone made her wonder what he'd sound like in bed. Except she shouldn't wonder about him naked and between the sheets because it wasn't going to happen. No way, no how.

"Well, if it led me here, to this moment, I'm okay with all that happened. I can't regret the chance to have dinner with such a beautiful and intelligent woman." He reached out and caressed her hand where it lay on the table.

Whoa.

The waiter appeared with dinner and fresh drinks. The server's timing couldn't have been better as far as Cassie was concerned.

They ate, talking about the challenges they each faced in running their respective businesses. Afterward, Trent talked her into sharing a dessert.

The crème brûlée arrived and he didn't hesitate to steal the extra spoon. "Relax, darlin', you'll get some." He flashed a devilish smile and his eyes sparkled.

She arched a brow at him and waited. Would he really try to feed her? Would she let him? Her answer came soon enough.

He spooned up a bit of the custard with the crispy sugar crust and aimed at her mouth. "Open wide, darlin'."

She shook her head, unable to control the twitch of her lips as she fought the giggle that welled up.

"Come on, now. Don't deny me this, open."

Cassie controlled the urge to respond. Fought hard against whatever it was about him that pulled at her.

"Cassie. Open. Now."

After a valiant struggle, she lost the fight and her lips parted as he slipped the spoon inside her mouth. What was it about this man that had her responding to his commands? Under normal circumstances she would have slapped her napkin down and walked away. She did not take orders from anyone.

"How is it?" His gaze held steady on her mouth, transfixed by her tongue sweeping out to clean up any remnants of the bite of custard.

"Delicious." When had her breathing become so labored?

34

"Yes. You are." He scooped up another bite and brought it to his own mouth. Cassie stared. Watching the strong chiseled jaw lower and take the bowl of the spoon inside. Right where she wanted to explore.

Okay. Now things were getting out of hand. She just met this guy. "How is it?"

Shit. Did she ask that?

He leaned in until his custard-sweetened lips were a hairsbreadth from the shell of her ear. She shivered. "Delicious. But I bet you're sweeter, Cassie."

He slipped his tongue out to trace the outer edge of her sensitive ear. Her panties flooded with desire as her nipples pebbled and cried out for similar attention. She groaned.

"Come back to my room with me, Cassie. Let me sip from those sweet lips, tease those beaded nipples, taste the nectar on your thighs."

"Yes." The word slipped out before she knew what she'd said.

Trent stood, grabbed the custard, grabbed her hand, and walked out of the restaurant.

"Room 128." He tossed over his shoulder as he passed the maître d' without slowing down.

On the short walk back to his room, Trent tried not to run. Fear that she'd change her mind before he got her alone gnawed at him. They stopped at his door and he let go of her hand to dig out the room key.

"Um, Trent." Her voice was soft, unsure.

"Don't change gears on me now, darlin'." He tried not to beg, but he was a hairsbreadth away from dropping to his knees for the first time in his life.

"I'm sorry, but I shouldn't do this. I can't explain what happened in there." Her face grew red again and she looked down at her boots.

He was pretty sure she knew what happened back in the dining room. With a single finger, he reached out and tilted her face up to his and stepped in close so their gazes locked. "Cassie, do I need to check out of the hotel so I'm no longer a guest? 'Cause I will if that makes you more comfortable. I can't explain it either, but I know I need to have you in my arms, need to taste your skin"—he dragged his finger along her jaw line, caressing the smooth skin—"feel you quivering with the pleasure I give you."

She groaned.

It was a gut-wrenching, guttural sound that was super sexy for the raw honesty of it. She wanted him as bad as he wanted her he just had to help her accept it.

"Is it terrible if I say yes?" A small smile kicked up the corners of her mouth.

"Not at all, darlin'. If you'll wait here, I'll grab my things and we can take care of checking me out. I do hope that means you're planning on lettin' me stay all night." He couldn't help but tease her a bit.

She laughed and flashed a naughty smile. "That's a risk you'll have to take, cowboy." In the blink of an eye, the confident sexy vixen was back and in control. "I'll go ahead and take care of your room. Meet you in the lobby in five minutes?"

"Sounds good. Just apply any charges to the card on record. I'll sign when I join you."

"No, sir. I'll take care of it." She turned to walk away.

"Cassie, absolutely not. I bought you dinner; you are not to waive any charges, do you understand me?"

"What'ch ya gonna do about it, cowboy?"

"There are always consequences, darlin'." he promised, letting a hint of darkness creep into his words. She had no idea she was playing with fire. He hadn't planned on introducing her to the pleasures of bondage and domination yet. It appeared his timetable might be moved up.

"Now that's a risk I'll just have to take, ain't it, cowboy?" she drawled and disappeared around the corner out to the lobby.

Trent entered his room, gathered the few things he'd brought along, and left the custard on a table along with a tip for the maid service. He hadn't used the room much, but that wasn't their fault.

Out in the lobby, he found Cassie waiting behind the reservation desk. She slid the zeroed-out bill over to him and pointed to the line at the bottom. "If you'll sign here, Mr. Jones, we're sorry for the trouble with your stay and your room. We do hope you'll come again and give us another chance to show you the excellent service we provide."

Trent gritted his teeth and grunted as he took the pen from the willful, taunting woman. Oh, she was asking for trouble, and he was without a doubt the one to dish it out. "I'm sure I'll be back to give your establishment another try. Quality service is always appreciated, and so far you've exceeded my expectations." He smiled as she blushed that hideous magenta color again.

"Let me show you out." She came around the desk and walked with him through the front doors. Outside, she grabbed his hand and tugged him to the left. "My cottage is this way, on the edge of the grounds."

"I asked you not to waive the fees, Cassie, and I promised consequences if you did it." He knew he sounded intimidating, and he tried to take the edge off it, but the woman provoked his dominant side. Would she be able to handle this aspect of him? They'd just met.

She glanced over at him and raised an eyebrow. "What, cowboy? You gonna tie me up and spank me for being a bad girl?"

His dick got hard just listening to her challenging taunt. "Yes." His voice came out gravelly, even to his own ears.

They stopped in front of a small cottage and she hesitated to open the door. "Trent, what're you saying exactly?"

Again, he reached out to caress the satin of her cheek. "I'm saying that yes I'd very much like to tie you up and spank that pert little ass of yours for misbehavin'." He sighed. "But I won't unless you're willing. I'm a dominant man, darlin'—I control things in the bedroom, and with the right woman, I'd be willing to extend that control outside the bedroom. It's not a requirement, but you need to understand that when we step inside your cottage, I'm running the show. If you are uncomfortable with something I'll give you a way to stop everything. Do you think you can handle that?"

She drew a deep breath. Stared into his eyes as though searching for something, some answer. He cursed himself for not telling her sooner, but he hadn't intended to let this side of himself loose with her. So he waited for her answer.

The tenseness in her face relaxed and a curious light sparkled in her eyes. "I think we'll manage, cowboy." And she opened the door.

# Chapter Three

Cassie hoped she hid the tremors in her hands well enough. Dear God, the man had looked and sounded like pure sin when he told her he wanted to tie her up and spank her. Damned if her already-soaked panties didn't get wetter. She'd always liked strong-willed men, confident men, but this verged into uncharted territory. Yet, her body seemed to catch on quicker than her mind had, and it was territory that intrigued her. She'd read her share of erotica and erotic romance over the years, but somehow she knew what this man was talking about would be in a different league altogether.

And the truth was she wanted—no, needed—to find out what he was promising.

He set his bag down on the couch and looked at her, really looked at her. "Strip."

She blinked.

"Cassie, there are a few ground rules here. First, when I give an order you follow it. Understand?"

She nodded.

"Second is, you will always give a verbal response to any question asked. You will answer and then add on sir at the end. In this case, the answer is yes, sir. Understand?"

"Y…yes, sir." Her heart pounded, almost drowning out his words.

"Third, if you need me to pause for a moment, say the word yellow. If you need me to stop and end the evening, say the word red. Do you understand?"

"Yes, sir."

"What are your safe words and what are they for, Cassie?"

"Yellow to pause, red to stop, sir."

"Very good, darlin'." He smiled at her, his praise washing over her like a soothing balm.

"Now, strip."

"Yes, sir."

She reached up and unsnapped the top of her shirt to reveal the sheer green bra she wore. Sexy undies gave her a sense of femininity even when wearing work clothes all the time. She went through them like crazy, but it was worth it for her self-esteem.

Next, she pulled off her boots and shimmied her jeans down to reveal the matching thong.

"Christ, woman, that is the sexiest underwear I've ever seen." He reached out to slide a finger under the mesh covering one breast. "It covers everything but hides nothing." He groaned.

"I'm glad you like it, sir." She reached behind her to remove the bra.

"No. Leave the underwear and bra on." His words rapped out in a commanding tattoo that had her dropping her hands without ever making a conscious decision to obey.

"Yes, sir."

"Have you ever had a lover spank you during sex, Cassie?"

"Once, sir." She watched him as he walked over to the bed and sat down.

"Come here, Cassie." He curled his finger to match his words.

"Yes, sir."

"Did you like it when he swatted your ass?"

Her breathing grew labored as she thought back to that moment. "No. Yes. Maybe." She stopped, took a breath, and decided to answer with more honesty than she ever had, even to herself. "Yes, sir. I liked it."

"You seem a little unsure, darlin'."

"I'm sure. I just..." She drew a steadying breath. "It surprised me at the time, and I acted like I didn't like it. Later, I didn't want to admit I liked it because it seemed shameful, sir."

"I see. Thank you for your honesty, Cassie. That is of great importance to me. I want nothing but honesty between us. It's the safe way for us to indulge in this kind of pleasure."

"Yes, sir."

"I do like how that sounds on your lips, darlin'. Now, bend over my knees." He helped her position her hips over his knees and draped the rest of her down either side of his legs. He placed a firm hand on her lower back to hold her in place. "I'm not going to tie you up tonight since we just met."

Disappointment lodged in her chest. That was a particular fantasy she had always wanted to live out.

"I am going to spank you as punishment for going against my wishes."

"But, I didn't know you'd be so unhappy, sir." She tried to raise her head up and he pressed down on her back, not letting her up.

"I told you there would be consequences. Now, you will count each of the ten strokes for me."

"Y...yes, sir." Nerves gripped her in a sudden and relentless stranglehold.

"Cassie, are you okay, darlin'? Do you need to use a safe word?"

She took a deep breath. No. Shoot, she needed to say it. "No, sir."

"Good girl." He landed the first swat.

Cassie jumped in surprise, but not pain. It was a light swat that warmed her left cheek a bit. "One, sir."

The next landed on her right cheek, similar power. "Two, sir."

The third had more sting to it. "Three, sir."

They increased in strength until she'd gotten to ten, at last. Her eyes watered, but she wasn't crying because it wasn't what she would call painful, more uncomfortable. Her bottom was warm and tingly and she was sure it had to be bright red from the swats.

"Very good, Cassie. Your ass is a lovely shade of pink now." He smoothed his hand over the warmth and she shivered from the sensation. "I took it easy on you since this was the first time. Be warned, I am not always so nice. I can and will spank you until you beg me to stop. Do you understand?"

"Yes, sir," she mumbled from under the mass of her hair that hung around her face.

"Good." He slid a hand between her thighs and past the elastic of her thong.

"Oh yes, that pussy is all wet. You liked that didn't you, Cassie?" His finger traced up and down her slit, dipping in and out of her juices.

"Yes, sir."

He plunged the teasing finger into her channel, pulled back, and plunged in again. "Oh, woman, you surely do test my powers of control. Do you know how bad I want to plow my cock into your tight, wet opening?" He added a second finger.

"Please, sir." She whimpered. She needed more than his fingers inside her, filling her.

"Please what, Cassie? Please add another finger? Please stop? Please plow my cock into your tight hole?"

She groaned, a low, needful sound. "Please, more. sir."

"More what, darlin'? You have to tell me what you want." His rich, whiskied tone strummed every vibrating nerve in her body, and her pussy clenched down hard on his fingers.

He withdrew in an instant. "Ah-ah-ah. No coming yet. Now tell me what you want."

She moaned and cried out in frustration. "You. Your mouth on me, your cock in me. Please, sir, for the love of God, fuck me!"

"Well, darlin', all you had to do was ask." She caught the flash of a grin as he lifted her and laid her on her back on the bed. He spread her thighs wide and knelt between them. "I love that you're shaved bare, darlin'. Makes it easier to get to the good parts." His tongue flicked out and slid past the crotch of her undies, which he held aside to allow him to delve between her swollen lips. He made a humming noise as he continued to lap at her with long, bold strokes that swept from her opening to her clit.

Pleasure rolled through her. "Mmmm..."

He pulled back, bringing the underwear down her thighs and off. Spreading her legs again, he resumed his ministrations. His tongue drove into her core, demonstrating what was to come. She ground against his mouth, needing more contact. He retreated to flick her clit. Her whole body shook with each warm, wet touch of his tongue. Her nipples pebbled and she gripped her bedspread in her fists. Like a leading rein snapping, her orgasm broke over her. Pleasure zapped along every nerve as he continued to lap at her clit and opening. He never stopped, never relented, as her release stretched out until it tapered to a perfect, bliss-filled end that left her floating.

He rose up and stood over her. "That is the sweetest damn pussy I've had in about forever. I could stay down there all night."

She chuckled. "You'd have to come up for air sometime, cowboy."

He didn't respond.

"Uh, I mean sir." Her face warmed.

"Better. And you're right. I would have to come up for air at some point." He grinned and stripped.

Cassie laid there enjoying the show as he pulled off the blue shirt and the T-shirt he wore beneath to reveal a firm, lightly defined torso. It was a working man's body, not a gym head's. He ditched his boots and jeans in short order, followed by his socks. His rock-hard cock jutted from the juncture of his thighs, the base surrounded by a trimmed thatch of dark hair. He was a good general length and thickness, and she was damn near desperate to have him buried inside her. He was sexy as hell.

Trent reached down and pumped his cock, relishing the freedom of bare skin. Considering he'd signed up for Soul Mates Dating as a lark, it was a pure stroke of luck that had such a beautiful woman spread out before him. He dug a condom out of his bag, rolled it on, and returned to the bed. She made a little moue of disappointment.

"What's wrong, darlin'?" He kneeled over her and traced her pouty lips with his fingertip.

"I'd intended to suck your cock. But you went and sheathed it before I realized what you were doing, sir."

"Oh, there'll be plenty of time for that later. Right now all I can think about is burying myself in your heat." He glanced at her wrought-iron headboard and sent up a prayer of thanks. "So grab the bars of your headboard and spread your legs like a good girl. And Cassie, do not let go or there will be consequences."

She nodded as she placed her hands on the cool metal.

He smacked the side of her thigh, just hard enough to make it tingle.

"Yes, sir."

"Better. Don't make me keep havin' to remind you, darlin'." He lifted one of her legs over his shoulder and pressed the tip of his cock to her opening. He slid inside and pushed, edging deeper into her heat in a slow, steady press. Seated hilt-deep, he took a big shuddering breath. "God, you feel good, Cassie. It's like you were made for me."

He withdrew to the thick rim of the head and surged back inside her warmth. With each thrust and retreat, he increased the pace and the power of his motion. Then her voice broke through and spurred him on.

"Harder, sir! More!" Her fevered demands fed his own pulsing need. He slammed into her body over and over again until his release loomed. Reaching down, he rubbed her swollen clit, circled it, and then stroked over it. The walls of her vagina clamped down on him spasmodically as her cries pierced the rhythmic slapping sound of their bodies joining. He could hold back no more and shouted his own pleasure as he lost control, surrendering to the stampede of his orgasm. Slowing his thrusts as they both returned to earth, he was torn between lying on her, covering her with his body as he wanted to do, and the fear his weight would be too much.

She took the decision out of his hands when she pulled him down on top of her. Brazen little vixen, she pleased him. After a few minutes of letting her stroke his back and butt, he pulled away to dispose of the condom. Back in bed, he rolled her to her side and curled his body around hers as though he might protect her from the world. She fit so naturally against him he had to control the urge to utter the declaration that rang in his head. *Mine* repeated as though on a loop in his brain, accompanied by images of their lovemaking.

"Mmm. I'm glad you like to snuggle." Cassie's tired voice floated up from the cloud of her hair.

"I'd still be inside you, joined to you, if I hadn't had to dispose of the condom. Sleep, Cassie, you'll need your rest for later." He couldn't cease smiling as he, too, drifted off to oblivion.

Trent woke to the most amazing sensation. The warm, wet caress of Cassie's mouth on his growing erection made it on the list—in record time—of the top five ways he liked to wake up. Having attained full cognizance, he thrust his fingers into her hair and guided her head. With a gentle thrusting motion he took control of the blowjob, but strong hands pressed against his hips and tried to wrestle it back.

"If you don't move your hands, darlin', I will restrain them." He made the promise knowing he had everything he needed nearby. A robe with a belt hung on a closet door a few short feet away.

She lifted her head. "But I want to pleasure you."

"I believe you forgot something."

"I di—oh. I want to pleasure you, sir. Please."

"You are, but I warned you that I will remain in control. Now, remove your hands or I will restrain them."

"Yes, sir." Much to his disappointment, she placed her hands on the bed, one on each side of his hips.

"That's it, darlin'."

She'd sucked him back into her mouth, working up and down his length. Dear heavens, she had skills. His hips thrusted over and over again with his hand back in her hair. Before long, her hands returned to his hips.

"I warned you." He pushed her back from his groin and stood up, then walked over to the robe. The belt slipped out of the loops easily.

She knelt on the bed watching him, wariness in her beautiful eyes.

"Hands behind your back." He nodded when she complied without comment. "Do you remember your safe words?"

"Yellow to pause, red to stop, sir."

"Very good, Cassie." He lashed the belt around her arms a few times, ensuring she would not wiggle out of the binding but not cutting off her circulation. With her secured, he tossed a pillow on the floor at his feet. "Now, climb down from the bed and kneel."

"Yes, sir." She awkwardly shifted onto her bottom before she scooted to the edge of the bed.

To kneel on a pillow with hands bound in back was tricky for even an experienced sub, so he helped her control her descent. He straightened up, pleased to realize she was the perfect height to kneel and take his cock in her mouth. She glanced up at him, her vulnerability etched across her face.

44

He reached out and stroked along her jaw. "You look beautiful, naked and bound for me." His erection throbbed in a needy, pulsing rhythm that had started as he wound the belt around her wrists and grown more intense with each loop up her forearms. He stroked himself, brushing his fingers over his length. "Do you see how hard you make me? How badly I want you?"

"Yes, sir."

"Open your mouth, darlin'." He slid his sensitive flesh past her lips and over her tongue, thinking this might be the closest to heaven he'd ever get. He eased into a steady pumping motion, working his cock in and out of her throat. She swallowed him expertly but not easily. Trent watched his length disappear into her mouth over and over, even as saliva dribbled down her chin.

Too near the edge, he withdrew. Her adorable little whimper of disappointment made him want to sink back into her mouth, but the desire for her heat to wrap around him overruled all other ideas. He helped her to her feet and led her back to the bed. After he tipped her across the mattress, facedown, he rubbed a hand over her backside. His fingers wandered and he stroked between the beautifully plump cheeks. She stilled but did not shrink away. He stepped back, grabbed a condom and lube from his bag, and then placed a few pillows under her hips to achieve the proper angle.

Cassie lay still as Trent spread her legs and knelt between them. Was she going to let him do this? So far, she'd allowed him complete and utter control. Relished his mastery even. But taking her virgin ass was not something she'd had planned.

Trent loomed behind her, encompassing the space around her. He stroked his hand over a globe of her ass and squeezed gently. His touch sent excitement skipping along her nerves even as it settled the turmoil in her mind. Somehow she connected to this man on an inexplicably elemental level. She trusted him not to hurt her physically or emotionally.

The cold wetness of the lube sent a shock through her system. She took a deep breath. She'd always wanted to do this, but she thought it would be with a steady partner, not a domineering cowboy who'd waltzed into her life.

She tensed as he rubbed his finger over her pucker. He backed off, continuing to smooth his free hand over her bottom.

He bit her.

As he sank his teeth into her cheek, he slid a finger past the tight ring of muscle. He was in, stretching her with the single digit. She breathed through the odd sensation, glad he had so cleverly distracted her.

"That's it, darlin', relax and let your body adjust." He resumed stroking her bottom. Then he pulled the finger out and slid it back home.

Oh my. That was nice.

He continued to work his finger in and out until all her nerves had fired up and were telling her this invasion felt good. As her hips pushed back into his thrusts, he added a second finger. The sense of fullness overwhelmed her, and she couldn't imagine taking his cock back there. Still gliding in and out of her backside, the pleasant sensations returned. A moan escaped.

"That's it baby, let me in. This is gonna be so good for both of us. I promise." His deep rumble, the want in his voice, almost undid her.

"Yes. More!" She heard herself answer.

A sharp smack on her ass jolted her memory while masking the addition of a third finger.

"Yes, sir," she corrected herself. So stretched. Her body adjusted, wanted more. Needed more. Her bottom pressed back, attempting to take more of his fingers inside. Then he spread the three fingers and reached around to rub over her clit, causing the world as she knew it to melt away.

Like a stampede, it started slow and worked up to a ferocious crash. She cried out his name, lost to everything but the presence of him in her body and the ripples of pleasure that streaked out from where they were joined.

"God, darlin', that was so fucking sexy." He rubbed his cock along her soaked cleft.

Still dazed, she managed a smile. His fingers slipped out and the wide head of his cock pressed against her still-spasming hole. He pushed in and the shock of it cleared the cobwebs.

Not his fingers.

She took a deep breath and pushed out against him with her muscles.

"Oh, darlin', you're so tight. So fucking tight." He continued to invade her body until she thought he would rip her in two.

Panic set in, her heart pounded, and her breath grew shallower and harder to draw in. "Yellow!"

"Okay. I got you. Take a minute. Let me know when you're ready to continue." He let his hand slide up over her hip to stroke along her spine in long, relaxing drags.

Cassie took a few deep breaths and realized her panic had gotten the best of her. She was fine. He was taking care of her even as he took his own pleasure. "Okay. I'm ready."

"You sure, darlin'?" He waited for her response.

"Yes, sir."

"Mmmm, I do like the sound of that." He resumed his inexorable advance deeper into her body. Then he was balls deep in her ass with his chest pressed against her back. "God, Cassie. Do you know how deep I am inside you? How tight and hot you are around me? It's like you're gonna set me on fire." The sexy words and the rasp of his voice pushed her past any lingering fear. He was right. He felt so good and she knew it would get better when he moved.

"Yes, sir. Please, sir, move." The pleading in her voice came as a surprise to both of them.

Beyond speech, he retreated and then gently slid back in. Tingles sizzled along her fired-up nerves and converged in her pussy. He increased the pace until he rammed into her in utter abandon. She met him thrust for thrust, reveling in the feel of him and the knowledge that she had driven him to this point.

He returned his hand to her swollen nub and stroked it. Cassie couldn't say what happened in exact detail, her world just imploded. She shattered around him, he cried out, and then she lay on the bed, covered by her cowboy, who was still buried in her body. She'd have sworn during the hazy aftermath of orgasm that she felt his heartbeat through their connection. But that was probably her being fanciful.

Trent rolled off her and tossed the condom. Returning to the bed, he carried a warm washcloth and cleaned her up. She lay replete and content to be ministered to. Done, he climbed back in bed and pulled her against him under the covers as the sun came up, invading their space.

"Thank you, darlin'. That was one of the most incredible nights of my life." He kissed her shoulder, letting his fingers drift over her skin.

"It was pretty fantastic." She sighed and let her eyes close.

"I'm not sure I can let you go, darlin'."

"Then don't," she mumbled and floated into the oblivion of sleep.

# Chapter Four

Trent woke to full morning sunlight streaming in on him. Alone. He listened for the shower, but silence reigned. Sitting up, he saw her clothes were gone and his were laid over a chair with his hat on top and his boots on the floor below. He got up, took a shower, and dressed. Still no Cassie. He decided to go look for her because they needed to talk. First, they needed to discuss the fact he did not like waking up alone, particularly after such an intimate night. And, second, they needed to figure out what was going to happen next. This—whatever it was between them—was not over by a long shot.

Trent wandered into the barn and found Cassie rubbing down one of the mares.

"Should've known I'd find you in the barn and not in the office."

After a pause in the stroke of the currycomb when he first spoke, she resumed the repetitive motion. "Oh? Why were you looking for me?"

"Because we have a few things to discuss. Why were you hiding from me?" He stepped into her personal space, placing his hand over hers on the comb. He brought the distracting movement to a halt.

"I wasn't hiding. I was giving you a chance to clear out, cowboy. No fuss, no muss." She slipped her hand out from under his and broke the contact.

"Clear out? What gave you the idea I might want to clear out?" Damn it, he'd told her last night he didn't want to let her go.

"A long history of love'em and leave'em cowboys. Then there's the obvious fact that you essentially signed up for a one-night stand last night, even if I'm not who the agency scheduled. And of course there's the plain truth that you have a ranch to run three hours from here, and I have the Mustang to manage. Even if we wanted to, it wouldn't work out between us based on distance alone."

Trent smiled. She wanted more badly, but she'd be a fool to get involved with a man so far away when her focus needed to be on her business. With a grunt that clearly said the hell with that, he spun her around and crowded her against the horse. "Cassie, don't lump me in with some list of anonymous assholes that didn't have the good sense to recognize a woman worth keeping when they saw her. As for last night's date. I'm damn glad that woman bailed on me since I got to meet you. And you are not a one-night stand. You are something indefinable that I wanted—no, had— to explore. And so you're aware, I ain't done exploring yet. Might not be for a long time."

He kissed her, took her mouth and claimed it as surely as he'd claimed her body the previous night. Breaking off the kiss before it turned into much, much more, he continued his rebuttal. "And finally, the distance issue can and will be worked out. For now, it's a short enough drive that I can come here for long weekends and leave my foreman in charge."

His intense gaze never left her as hopefulness blossomed into joy beneath her ribs. "You'd drive that far just to see me?"

"Darlin', I'd drive a hell've a lot farther to see you. And for the promise of sinking into your welcoming heat? I'd go to hell and back."

Cassie wanted to hit herself in the head for acting a fool. The man had said he didn't want to let her go, but she figured it'd been a dream when the soft words sounded. "Take me back to the cottage, cowboy. I need your skin against mine, and I don't need any employees catching me in the buff."

"My pleasure, darlin'." He scooped her up and tossed her over his shoulder. With one hand wrapped around her thigh, placing his fingers flush up against her heated pussy, and the other hand firmly on her ass, she had no choice but to hang there and hope they didn't run in to anyone.

Fate could be an ornery bitch.

Ted, the night manager, passed them on the path as he headed to his car. "Hi, boss."

She heard the smirk in his voice before she caught a glimpse of his face.

She made sure to shoot him the you-say-anything-and-you're-dead look from under the curtain of her hair. As he guffawed loudly, she was pretty sure he'd ignored the look, if he'd even seen it.

Alone in the cottage, Trent lowered her down. Eager to get his hot flesh and hard muscles under her fingertips, she reached for his shirt.

"Not quite yet, darlin'." He grabbed her hands, stopping her progress.

"What? We can talk some more later, cowboy."

"And we will, but first we have some business to attend to. Last night's ground rules are still in effect, and you left the bed without permission this morning. I owe you a spanking."

"Excuse me?" Cassie's blood, pumped by her pounding heart, rushed through her body and muffled his words. But she heard enough to gather that he was serious. Last night wasn't just fun and games? He was like this all the time?

She paused as images of their night flickered across her mind's eye like a slide show. Her soaked panties got wetter as she thought about surrendering control to such a caring and attentive lover.

He sat on the end of the bed. "Strip and come here, darlin'."

Although she enjoyed the surrender, the punishments were not high on her list of things to do. Regardless, Trent didn't look as though he would be persuaded from his course of action. "Yes, sir."

With quick, efficient motions, she shed her shirt, jeans, and boots. Today she wore a black lace bra and thong, one of her favorite sets.

"God, you do have the best underwear, woman. Leave them on. The thong won't be a hindrance to your spanking, and I bet your cheeks will look sexy glowing red against the black lace."

She crossed the room on leaden feet.

"Come on now, it's not that bad, darlin'. Besides, the quicker you get over here, the quicker it'll be over."

She draped herself over his knees, then waited for the first blow. It came, a sharp smack to her left cheek followed by a matching one to her right. Then he laid even blows down the middle of her backside from the top of her rump to where the cuff of her ass met her thighs. Four more on alternating cheeks and she was sore and squirming.

"Now, darlin', why are you being spanked?" He smoothed his hand over her flaming-hot bottom.

"I left the bed without your permission, sir."

"Are you sorry you left me alone with no way to slake my morning desire but to take a lonely shower?"

The image of him as he stood in the spray of the shower with his cock in his hand nearly undid her. "Yes, sir."

His hand wandered between her legs to stroke the lacy crotch of her undies. She knew without a doubt what he would find.

"Someone likes having her butt warmed. Your pussy seems to be awfully wet." He slid two fingers past the elastic band and into her heat.

She tried to hold still, to not push back into his hand. She commanded her body not to do it, and yet she found herself wiggling backward. "Please, sir. More."

"Oh, darlin', I promise there will be more." He added a third finger.

Her hips ground into his hand and she moaned. Then he added the stimulation of his thumb to her clitoris, causing her to buck like a wild bronco. He pressed down on her back, holding her still as she burst. Her orgasm came as a short, sharp explosion that let her down as quickly as a ton of bricks.

Trent gazed at Cassie standing before him, clad in two miniscule scraps of lace, and experienced a surge of male satisfaction followed rapidly by a knee-buckling possessiveness. Good thing he was sitting down. He'd been crazed as he traipsed all over the resort looking for her. Disbelief over the fact she'd ditched him after everything they'd done and shared had added fuel to the fire. Of course, once he found her and figured out what she was thinking, he calmed down.

For the most part.

He would help her understand that he wasn't clearing out, that he'd be there for her. It might take some time, but he figured he might as well get started. An untrained submissive, she had a lot to learn about giving up control and trusting him to both be there and take care of her. He spied the uncertainty lurking in her gaze as she waited for his command. Well, it was a start.

"Darlin', come here, please."

She stepped closer to him so that she stood between his knees. Tiny tremors had her whole body vibrating.

"Are you cold, honey?"

"No, sir."

"Nervous?"

"A little, sir."

"Scared?" He tried to keep his brows from drawing together.

"A little, sir." The shaking increased a bit with this admission.

He pulled her into his arms, caressing her back as he pressed his cheek against the slight curve of her belly. "Shh… darlin'. Do you know that I would never harm you in any way?"

"Yes, sir." Her lips moved against his head where her face rested on his hair. Her arms had wrapped around his upper shoulders and head.

"Then what scares you? Is it something I've done?"

"No, not physically." She hesitated and he waited, hoping she would elaborate. "I'm scared of how much I like giving you control, that I like being spanked, and, most importantly, I'm scared at how much I like you when I don't even know you."

Trent took a deep, thankful breath. She liked him. He grinned so big he thought his face might split. "Oh, you sweet, amazing woman. Thank you for telling me that. I want you to always be able to tell me how you're feeling or what you're thinking. I'm glad you like what we've been doing together, but this is all new to you. Give yourself some time to become accustomed to how we play. It may all seem strange and a bit scary for a while, even if you like it. That's part of what the safe words are for. Okay?"

"Yes, sir. Thank you for understanding." She squeezed him.

"As for us, I like you too, Cassie. A lot. And this thing between us is moving fast. If it makes it any better, it scares me a little too." He pulled back and smiled at her. "But I intend to see if this is leading where I think it is. You should know that eventually I expect we'll end up married, or at least together forever."

"You do?"

He didn't think she could be any prettier, but he was wrong. Her face lit up with such pleasure that it made his heart ache from want of bursting from happiness. And to his great relief, her trembling had stopped.

"I do, darlin'. I'm glad to see that makes you happy instead of sending you running for the hills."

"I'll never run from you again, cowboy. I'm sticking around to see how this ends. Speaking of endings, I believe we have some unfinished business, sir."

"I believe we do. On your knees, woman, I want to sink my cock into that delicious mouth of yours."

"Yes, sir. She lowered down and opened his jeans to release his growing erection.

He sank into her waiting mouth, relishing the warm, wet slide. A few strokes between her lips, and he realized he wouldn't last long like this.

"Darlin', I need to be inside you. Let me go." He withdrew, grabbed a condom from his pocket, and shed the rest of his clothing. "Lose the lace. I want you naked." The joy of her ready acceptance of his direction and her eagerness to please rolled over him.

This woman was everything he'd ever wanted and a few things he'd never imagined.

"On the bed, on your back. Legs spread."

"Yes, sir." She lay on the bed naked and waiting.

He crawled between her legs and lifted them over his shoulders before plunging deep inside her. He wanted to be so deep in her that there'd be no telling where one stopped and the other started.

As he pumped into her throbbing heat, he knew he'd come home. He slipped a finger between them and flicked her clit with a ruthless determination to see her explode. "That's it, darlin', come for me. Come for me now!" He willed it with every fiber of his being, every blood-engorged inch of his cock, but mostly with his whole heart.

She groaned in frustration as her hips rose to meet his. "I'm so close. Please, sir!"

"Oh god, Cassie. It makes me so hot and hard when you call me sir." He smiled as her breathing grew harsh. "That's it, let it go for me. Come for me, darlin'."

And she did.

Her pussy spasmed around his cock with enough force to level him if he'd been on his feet. She squeezed him as his own release careened through him, swamping him with sensory overload. His balls were too tight, her pussy too hot wrapped around his dick, and the sunlight too bright as his cum shot out in a shocking blast of pleasure.

He collapsed on top of her, exhausted by the powerful orgasm. After a few moments, he realized he was crushing her into the bed. "Sorry, darlin'. Didn't mean to squash you." He rolled off her and got up to get rid of the condom. "You okay?"

"Better than okay. Okay doesn't even scratch the surface." Her eyes sparkled with pleasure, and dare he say love? He hoped so, because he'd figured out he was already a goner.

"Glad to hear it. Mighty glad to hear it." He smiled and kissed her with every ounce of love he had tucked away for one day real soon.

# A Cowboy's Christmas Wish

*One Night With A Cowboy*
Book 3
**Sorcha Mowbray**

# Chapter One

Ford closed the back door, muffling the racket created by three sugar jacked kids, two barking dogs, and the rest of the Grayson clan. He drew a breath of clean, crisp winter air and held it until he had to release. His grip tightened on his keys as he headed to his truck.

The black paint gleamed in the moonlight, a welcoming sight. Why he'd agreed to spend the holidays with the entire Grayson family eluded him at the moment. Normally he spent the last two weeks of each year on a tropical island with at least one beautiful woman on his arm. Except that one year he'd found an accommodating set of friends. Whew, that had been a hell've a Christmas and New Year's.

He slid behind the wheel of his new F-150 Raptor—if his name hadn't been a family heirloom passed down over a hundred and fifty years, he'd have changed it when he came of age. With the push of a button on his key fob, the engine roared to life. The rumble of the truck comforted him. His first Ford hadn't purred like this one, but the hum of power was familiar.

He backed out of the driveway and pulled down the street. With a simple command, the nav unit woke up and awaited his request. He asked for the closest bar, and a moment later the smooth voice suggested The Silo, off Interstate 35. He shrugged, asked for directions, and then requested the radio be turned on. As the music poured through his speakers he grabbed his favorite ball cap off the seat and planted it on his head. The tattered hat bore his high school logo and had been a favorite since the day Melissa settled it on his head for the first time. He'd just made varsity football, and her eyes had shone with pride and genuine excitement for him. Melissa Adams turned out to be the biggest mistake of his life—well, his idiotic decision to dump her his freshman year of college was. Full of youthful arrogance, horny, and the newest stud on the University of Texas campus, he lasted three months before he cut her loose. Her cold acceptance of his decision only confirmed for him that he'd made the right choice at the time.

The navigation unit announced he'd arrived at his destination. He pulled in to the almost empty parking lot of a building with a grain silo sitting on top. The Silo was painted on the towering structure in bold black lettering. He shut off the truck and wandered inside. To his surprise, the interior had a modern feel with small accents here and there that spoke to farm life, an odd mix of rural and city. Over the speakers Luke Bryan sang about dropping everything for a girl.

Ford snorted. *If only I'd learned that lesson a little sooner.*

Over the din of the song and a smattering of murmured conversations, a female voice sliced through his musings. "Last call is in fifteen minutes."

The familiar voice caught his attention and drew his gaze to its source like a lode stone. Holy shit. What were the odds that the very object of his wistful musings would appear as though he'd conjured her from thin air, or maybe it was a Christmas miracle.

He gathered his scattered thoughts together and ambled up to the bar. He took his time, drinking in the sight of the woman, there in the flesh. Her long brown hair had streaks of red in it, the natural kind that came from genetics and not hair dye. The black tank top she wore had The Silo splashed across it in white lettering, and hugged her ample curves. Without a glance in his direction she asked, "What'll you have?"

"Brewmeister." Had his voice cracked? Maybe not, she never glanced up from washing the glasses in the sink.

"Coming right up." She turned around, slid open the top of the beer cooler, and bent over.

Ford's heart skipped a beat. Damn, she still had a great ass. Two soft, luscious globes made for a man's hands. He licked his dry lips and studiously ignored the throb between his legs.

She popped the top on the bottle and set it on the bar while she simultaneously tossed the cap into the garbage. "Two doll—" she stopped talking as their gazes collided.

Shit, he'd forgotten how blue her eyes were. It felt like he might fall and drown in them. Blue like the Caribbean Sea, they ranged from deep turquoise to bright aqua.

His pulse sped up, matching the pounding ache that now resided in his balls. She was a little older, and in some ways more stunning, than she'd been in high school.

Melissa's panties were damp. Had she peed herself or was that just a burst of lust bum-rushing her? Since incontinence wasn't an issue it had to be lust, which would make sense with Ford Grayson standing in her bar. It had to be him, if not she had finally cracked and was now having full-fledged hallucinations.

*Please, God, let it be him.* "Ford?" Had he heard her? She wasn't sure she'd spoken loud enough to be heard over the music, but since air refused to enter her lungs talking had become difficult. Standing, too, for that matter.

"Hi, Mel." He gave her that trademark Ford grin.

Without warning her body unseized and air rushed back in while spots danced before her eyes, obstructing her view. She found her voice again as she leaned on the bar for support. "What the hell are you doing here?"

He flinched and then shrugged. "Having a beer."

Having a beer? Seriously? The one that got away. The one that dumped her and left her to rot in Small Town USA was standing in her bar three days before Christmas and just having a beer? No way. This was fate giving her a chance at retribution.

"Well, two dollars." She turned her back and drew a breath as she collected herself.

"How've you been, Mel?"

She turned back around. "Just great, Ford. Everything's coming up roses." She went back to washing glasses.

The drunk at the end of the bar called out, "Hey honey, get me another cold one."

With a sigh Melissa looked at Cletus and knew he was done. But, she also knew he had nowhere to go and nothing to do tonight. She poured him a mug of coffee and walked down to where he sat.

"Clete, have some coffee. It's almost Christmas and I don't wanna have to call Maisey to come and get you."

The grizzled old man nodded and took the mug from her.

Satisfied he wouldn't be beyond stumbling up the block to get home, she returned to the sink. Ford was still there, damn him.

"So, you got out of Tuckerville." He half smiled even as his gaze ate her up. Or was she just imagining that?

"Not like I went far. Austin's only an hour away and, well, I didn't exactly make it big." She spread her arms wide and indicated the bar around her. "But I survived."

"Yeah, I can see that." He paused. "You look good."

"Thanks. You, too." She played it casual when all she wanted to do was crawl across the bar and lick him from head to toe. Apparently her libido didn't give two shits about revenge. How did he do this to her after all these years? After all the boyfriends and an ex-fiancé?

She glanced at the clock and realized she was five minutes late for last call. "That's it, folks. Last call."

Mel moved up and down the bar, filled last orders, closed tabs, and then shut down the register. By the time she looked up again, it was just after two in the morning, and everyone but Harold, one of her regulars, and Ford had gone. "Night, Harold. I'll see you later."

"You all right, Mel?" He looked meaningfully at Ford, who remained at the bar with his beer bottle in his hand.

"Yeah, I'm good. He's an old friend."

"If you're sure. Have a good one." Harold winked and eased off the stool that retained an imprint of his ass.

A minute later, it was just her and Ford left in the empty bar. The jukebox kicked on the next song and Janna Krammer's "Why Ya' Wanna" blasted over the speaker system. Mel's cheeks heated up, but she turned around and worked on wiping down the back bar.

"Mel." Ford's warm bass carried across the small space and caressed her skin.

"What do you want, Ford?" She threw down her rag and braced her hands against the bar top. Need pulsed thickly through her veins and pooled between her thighs. "What do you want from me? Why are you here?"

"Do you still think about me the way I think about you?" His gaze held a glimmer of vulnerability as he reached up and pulled the brim of his cap down low on his forehead.

Janna sang the very words on Mel's mind. Why'd she keep wanting him?

The silence drew out as she stared hard at the oak bar top and tried to form a response that didn't include either crawling across the bar and tackling him or slapping him so hard he landed on his well-formed ass. At the moment it was a toss-up which one she'd go with.

"No." Because there was no way he thought of her with the desire and need she still had for him. After almost ten years she must have faded into a sweet memory of his youth and not the lust fueled fantasy that haunted both dreams and fantasy. If she believed otherwise, she'd have no defense. No way to protect herself.

"Really? Not even an occasional 'what if' thought? What if I hadn't broken it off with you? What if I hadn't gone away to college? Maybe, what if I had asked you to marry me?" His deep, warm voice tormented her with every scenario she'd concocted since he'd called and broken it off with her. Then her mom had died, and she had nothing left after she worried about the next day's survival. With the memory of being deserted at the worst possible moment in her life, her anger resurged and dampened her desire.

"Wow. You must think a lot of yourself to believe I've had time in the last ten years to moon over you." She walked to the other end of the bar and started flipping off the lights that illuminated the bottles, the glassware, and even the coolers.

"What if I told you I jerk off at least four nights a week to memories of you that I stored away from our time together?"

"I'd say you need to get laid." She slid out from behind the bar and swept the floor. Of all the places in Austin, Ford Grayson had to come walking into The Silo and sit down? Why couldn't he go away? And damn it, why was this song still on?

# Chapter Two

F ord crossed the distance between them, cock hard and balls aching. Nothing about Mel didn't rock his world—even after ten years. Her body had softened and filled out in all the right places. Her eyes tracked his every move with a wary vulnerability that tore at his soul. "Even if you were right, and truth be told you probably are, nobody would do but you."

"Give over." She pushed him away. "I'm not that same starry-eyed girl you dated back in high school. You wanna get laid? I might be willing to accommodate you. But, if I do it will be on my terms." She folded her arms across her ample breasts and stared him in the eyes.

His cock thickened and lengthened at the prospect she might strip off her tight tee-shirt and tiny little shorts for him. Suddenly, she was the answer to every Christmas wish he'd made for the last nine years. Every fantasy he'd tried to live out in the tropical heat this time of year.

"Mel." He managed to push her name over the sandpaper that lined his throat. Saliva wouldn't answer his body's demand, and breath barely squeezed past the constriction in his airway.

She pressed a finger to his lips. "Don't. It's the holidays, and the truth is I don't want to face my lonely apartment. So, if you want me, I'm willing to oblige both our curiosities about what it was like and if it could possibly be everything we remember."

Relief sliced through his tension and let anticipation bubble to the surface. He slid his hands up over her shoulders and then her cheeks to cup her face as he possessed her mouth. The very same mouth that had led him to believe all was well with her. His tongue delved past her lips and teeth to explore her mouth in wild abandon.

With a groan, she clutched at his waist and pressed her breasts against his chest. In that moment Ford knew no business deal, no cattle auction, no rodeo win could ever compare with the exhilaration he got from tasting Mel. She was addictive.

He walked her backwards until they hit the pool table. In the space of a heartbeat, he shifted his hands from her face to her waist so he could lift her onto the sturdy surface. Her legs spread, welcomed him in as he pressed closer. He let his fingers drift under the hem of her tank top to tease the silky skin shielded from his view.

Their lips parted and he let the oxygen filter into his lungs to feed the hungry cells in his body with at least a small part of what they needed. A moment of clarity swept through his lust-fogged brain as he questioned how quickly they'd jumped from *hello* to *let's get naked.*

"You sure you want this? It's been a long time. A lot of things left unsaid, and a few that maybe should've stayed that way." He worked hard to not sink his fingers into the softness of her hips as he waited for her to answer.

"Cowboy, you always did talk too much." She reached up, pulled him down, and devoured him again. Her lips melded with his, tongues twined, and breath mingled.

The ability to think about anything but the taste of the woman in his arms escaped him as his world narrowed down to the fiery female who threatened to incinerate him with desire.

Mel whimpered as he shook off whatever gentlemanly notions had surged to the fore and he returned her kiss with a fervor that matched her own. Yeah, she wanted him, wanted this. She also had every intention of kicking him out the moment they were done and dismissing him with the callous disregard he had once shown her.

For now, she meant to enjoy his touch. Soak up the pleasure, the likes of which she had not experienced since the last time she was in his arms. Even as inexperienced kids, the sex had been special. Different. She just hadn't known that until the first time she slept with a man other than Ford. The whole experience had been like dropping into an ice bath after being in a sauna.

Sure, she'd had better lovers since that first clumsy post-Ford attempt, but even the good lovers hadn't compared. Now she needed to know if her memory was real or just the idealization of what she'd never have again.

So far, she'd been spot on.

His fingers teased up her midriff, bunching cotton on their way to her breasts. And God, did she want his hands on her breasts. Pinching, plucking, and teasing her nipples. His mouth sucking, biting, and licking the distended nubs. She bit back a whimper of need. Shit, it had been too long since her last lover. Six months was the longest dry spell she'd had since she gave up on Ford's return.

That had taken two years to accomplish. The night of her mother's funeral she'd gone out, gotten stinking drunk, and taken the first cowboy she found to bed. Hell, they'd never made it outta his truck. It wasn't pretty, didn't mean a damn thing, and had been a disaster. But, it got her past the point of hoping that the one man she wanted would come for her.

Now she would come for him. Again and again if the promises he made with his kisses were to be believed. Her shirt slipped up over her head and off her hands before he tossed it aside. She dropped her hands to his waist and reached for the button of his jeans.

He grabbed her hands. "Oh no, darlin'. If you touch me, this will be over way sooner than either of us wants."

"Ford, I wa—"

"Mel, I'm serious. If you can't keep your hands to yourself I will tie you up like a prize heifer, and then I'll have all night to torture you with pleasure." The bass of his voice rumbled through her chest as he pressed against her.

Her heart skipped several beats. The notion he might tie her up had her thighs clenching and her panties getting damper than they already were—which was pretty damn hard to imagine since she was soaked. Christ, the man had gotten better with age. She had no doubt he would do as he said. The promise lit his eyes with an unholy desire that threatened to consume every intention she had of kicking him out. If he was that good, how would she ever let him go again?

The silence stretched taut between them until he released her hands and refocused on her breasts. "Damn, your tits have only gotten better." He occupied each of his hands with her silk-covered flesh. "It's like they were made to perfectly fill my hands."

She looked down to see his huge, sun-browned hands cupping her breasts and couldn't resist thrusting forward. More. She needed more.

"I know, darlin'. I need it, too." And then, as though he'd read her mind, he had the cups of the bra shoved below her mounds and his mouth latched on to her right nipple. With his other hand, he teased and plucked at her left tip until she could no longer control herself. She whimpered with desire and arched into him with little thought for how needy she sounded and looked.

He switched to her other breast with his mouth and placed his fingers on the wet tip he had abandoned. Zings of pleasure darted from her breasts to her pussy, which now throbbed with an alarming level of lust driven pleasure. This was how a woman could come purely from a man's mouth on her breasts. She'd never felt this amount of crazed hunger before.

She reached up and gripped his shoulders as though hanging on for dear life. He moaned as he sucked on the distended peak of her nipple, and she couldn't take it anymore. She needed him naked and his cock buried deep inside her before her head exploded.

She pushed him away from her breast, taking him by surprise. Then she reached up, grabbed the sides of his shirt, and yanked with all of her might. Buttons popped and his shirt hung open as she growled in frustration. Where was the sexy sun-bronzed skin she had anticipated? The miles of muscle etched flesh for her delectation? *Not here.* She growled. In its place she found a fucking t-shirt. If she could have accomplished it, she would have ripped the offending cotton from his body. Instead she was stunned as she found herself quickly spun around and bent over the pool table with her hands gathered at the small of her back.

"I warned you about touching me," Ford ground out as he wrenched her shorts open and then pulled them to her ankles. A loud groan sounded from behind her—loud enough she heard it over her pounding heart—as cool air hit the heated flesh of her backside. "A thong? Woman you do know how to make it hard for a man to think."

Then, with no warning, his hand smacked down on her left cheek. Mel pressed her face against the soft felt over the slate surface of the pool table and tried to shut out the flashes of her fantasy come to life. How many times had she dreamed of being spanked? Of having her backside warmed just before a thick long cock drove into her from behind?

Three more smacks rained down on her bottom, evenly distributed across her rapidly heating cheeks. Her breath hitched and the first tremors of her orgasm rippled through her body. The smell of Ford—leather, man, and musk—wrapped around her and she was lost. She cried out as he landed two more blows and then he was between her legs, thong shoved aside, with his tongue thrust into her wet slit as she rode her orgasm through one peak and into a second.

Through it all her hands remained locked in his grip and pressed into her back as he lapped and licked her desire from between her thighs. He groaned again as she continued to seep moisture into his mouth. Then, with a gentle kiss to her labia, he rose up and released her hands. "Damn, Mel. You taste as sweet as I remember."

She pushed up from the pool table, stepped out of her shorts, and faced him. Her juices coated his lips and, with her backside still hot from his spanking, she wanted to climb that man and lick him clean. Her body reeled from the pleasure he'd delivered while her mind tried to sort out how he'd discovered her darkest fantasies. She'd never let herself acknowledge the truth, that the star of her erotic dreams had always been Ford.

But, after having had one of the tamer ones brought vividly to life, ignoring the truth grew very hard. Not unlike the man before her. She reached for him, but he stopped her with a gentle grasp on her wrists. "Darlin', look at me."

She lifted her gaze to his face and tried to hide her secrets from him. Would he be disgusted by her? By the pleasure she found when his palm heated her butt? By her need to give up control?

"Are you all right, darlin'? Did I…" He took a breath and forced the words past stiff lips. "Did I hurt you? I'm so sorry I let that go too far. I lost my head when you ripped my shirt off." Guilt swirled through him and churned in self-disgust. He knew better than to play those kinds of games with a girl like Mel.

Those were the kinds of games he played in tropical settings with experienced women, and only when he knew they were equally into it. He was no Dom, didn't really think much about kink as a general rule. He liked to be in control, discipline was a concept he'd grown up with, and well he was a rancher. Rope was an innate part of his daily life.

"Hurt me?" Mel sounded confused and a little dazed after the explosive orgasm—no, *orgasms*—he'd given her. A small burst of manly pride settled in his chest and eased some of his worry. Maybe she hadn't been as repulsed by his actions as he first thought. Now that he'd had a minute to think about it, she'd been as turned on as him and things had only escalated when he spanked her. In fact her, first orgasm had started before he even touched her pussy.

"Yeah, are you okay? With what just happened?" He waited and rubbed her wrists and arms as though gentling a skittish calf.

She hesitated, chewed her lower lip as though deciding how much to say. "I'm okay. You aren't—" She stopped drew a breath and started again. "How did you—"

"Shhh. Stop. I didn't know anything. You aren't upset with me for spanking you?"

She laughed. "Upset? God, Ford. It was like you knew. Like you reached in my head and dug out one of my deepest fantasies."

His cock throbbed in accord with her dark desires. She liked being spanked, huh? He could certainly work with that. He dragged her into his arms and kissed her. She moaned a long, low sound, achy with renewed need. He had to pull away and take a deep breath. Then her hands scrabbled at his belt buckle again.

"Darlin', I told you no touching me," he warned, his own need to come simmering like a volcano about to spew.

"But, that was before." She stopped and looked up at him.

He fell into her blue gaze until she renewed her efforts. "I warned you." He pulled off his shirt, flipped her around, and bent her over the pool table again. Using his long sleeved shirt, he bound her wrists behind her before turning her back around to stand.

Her eyes glazed over with a look he'd only ever seen from one woman. She had been a true, died in the wool submissive. They'd spent a few hot nights together and then moved on because he couldn't fulfill all her sexual needs. As a masochist she needed more pain in the long run than he could comfortably dish out. A good man knew his limits.

Could Mel be submissive? His little firebrand? She'd always given him hell when she deemed him out of line. Right up until the day he'd broken it off with her. Shit, she'd still stood up to him earlier when he'd strolled in. No, she might like this in the bedroom, but he doubted it went much further than that. Sexual submission he could handle. If he was honest, he could more than handle it. He downright looked forward to it. "Now, it's time for a little more fun."

# Chapter Three

Mel wanted to beg for more. More fun. More cock. More Ford. She wanted all of it more than she wanted to take her next breath, except if she didn't breathe she wouldn't get to enjoy any of it, would she?

Ford glanced around the bar. He spotted a club chair in the corner and led her over, hands still bound at her back. He helped her get settled so that her stomach rested over the back of the chair with her knees on the seat cushion.

"Very nice, darlin'." He circled around the chair and stopped behind her. "A little wider." He nudged her legs until her knees were braced against the sides of the chair.

He stroked her back, over her warm butt cheeks, down the backs of her legs. She relaxed and waited to see what would come next. He placed a kiss on each cheek of her ass and then slid his tongue along her wet folds. She tried to press into the wet heat of his mouth, but he pulled away. "Please." The word slid past her mental defenses to reveal how hot for him she was.

He moved around to where her head hung, with her hair trailing down her face. He lifted her head until she looked up at him and their gazes locked. "Please, what? Tell me what you want, what you need."

He sounded as desperate as she felt. "Your cock. Please." The words broke from her as she wiggled against nothing. Despite the two orgasms, she needed to feel him inside of her, filling her up.

"My cock, where? Where do you want it?" His voice rasped out of him with a sexy, grated sound that sent shivers cascading through her body.

"My pussy. Please, Ford."

Oh, thank heaven, he finally unbuckled his belt. She licked her lips as her vagina clenched with need. Without a word he slid his t-shirt off and bared his naked chest to her. His torso rippled with muscles—not ridiculously cut, but defined, undulating mounds of flesh that made her want to trace each ridge with her tongue.

"I promise you, I will give you what you need. Just not yet." The greedy glint in his eye warned her he was only getting warmed up. He opened his jeans and pulled out his dick.

Transfixed by the length and girth before her, she watched as he moved toward her. The tip leaked clear pre-come that had her licking her lips and sticking her tongue out to taste it. He stopped just short of letting her have what she wanted. Like a kid in a candy store, her wants and needs skipped around to what was most accessible. Her empty, aching pussy forgotten, she suddenly had to have his cock in her mouth.

"Is this what you want? You wanna suck my dick, darlin'?" He stroked it from root to tip and thrust his hips forward with little jerky movements.

"Oh, yeah. I want to suck your dick until you're cross-eyed." She'd never spoken like that with him before—hell, she'd never said anything like that, except in her fantasies.

Ford growled and surged forward until the head of his cock pushed against her lips and demanded entrance. She opened, willingly lapped at the tip, and then sucked the rest of him down. Mouth stretched until it ached and air cut off, she swallowed until he was lodged in the top of her throat. His sac bumped her chin and he threaded his fingers into her hair and squeezed against her scalp.

"Holy shit." The whispered words were reverent as he pumped into her mouth with little thrusts over and over.

Hands bound, all she could do was open wide and try to breathe through her nose. This demanding side of Ford was not one he had shown her when they were younger. But it resonated inside her—answered the call of the damsel deep in her soul who needed to let go of the reins and let someone else lead.

He pulled back, slid out of her mouth, and let her breathe. Then he shoved right back in to the hilt. "That's it, baby. Take it. Take all of that dick in your sweet little mouth."

The dirty talk cranked up the ache between her legs and had her squirming to soothe the throb. Then he slipped from her lips and disappeared. He nudged her opening and stopped with a growl. "Condom. I don't have a fucking condom."

Need overrode her caution, besides this was Ford. "I'm clean and on the pill."

"Me, too. Are you sure about this?"

Desperation laced his every word and made her more certain of her choice. Besides, wasn't it a little late to worry about disease after she'd sucked his cock like a lollipop? "Fuck me. Now."

With little warning, he drilled his cock into her pussy in a single powerful stroke that zinged to her nipples and beyond. Her body shook with the intensity of what he made her feel, both physically and emotionally.

"God damn, your pussy is so hot, darlin'." He slid out and then sank back in. He did it again, and then he pulled out and came back around to her head. He grabbed her hair and tilted her face up. "Open wide."

Her own tangy desire slid over her tongue as he sank his cock into her mouth. He shuddered as she swallowed his length. He pumped in and out of her mouth and then switched back to her pussy.

He sank into her heat and grabbed her hair in his fist again. The tug on her scalp as he fucked her pushed her past caring about how she looked or sounded. "Yes," she cried out as his thighs slapped against her own.

He continued working in and out of her body, and then with his free hand he reached down and pinched her clit. She exploded around him, spasmed in a furious clench and release cycle and sucked his own orgasm from his body. As her body's pleasure ebbed, he pulled from her and spilled his seed over her ass. The hot splash of his cum sparked a residual flash of desire as he rubbed his dick across her skin.

Her backside, still faintly pink from his spanking, glistened with his load where he had actually rubbed it in as though marking his territory. Christ, what had he done? She wasn't his. He'd given her up like a fool.

"Hang on, darlin'." He reached up and untied her hands, then used the shirt to wipe her off. He tucked himself back into his jeans, then helped her stand up. Her legs wobbled and she grabbed onto his arms to steady herself. With a curse, he hauled her close and kissed her.

He couldn't get enough of the woman. Every fantasy, every memory paled in comparison to the reality of having her in his arms, of tasting her, touching her—loving her.

Shit. He'd known it was a risk, but as soon as he'd clapped eyes on her he'd also known it was one he would take. Truth be told, he'd never stopped loving her, so it wasn't like he instantly fell in love. He realized within weeks of breaking it off what a fool he'd been. But, it took him a while to man up enough to try and fix his mistake.

It was past time to set things to rights. He scooped her up and sat down in the club chair. He cursed himself. "Mel, I need to say some things to you. And then it's up to you where we go from here." He settled one hand on her hip and the other arm curved behind her shoulders. "You're right, I've had my pick of women over the years. But, the truth is, when it's not the person you love in bed with you, none of it makes a bit of difference."

A new song came on and after a few bars of music Blake Shelton's voice crooned through the empty bar. Listening to the song of lost love found again in "Austin," Ford took heart. He stared at the woman who had haunted him for ten years. With the last line of the chorus he leaned in to kiss her.

She held her body stiffly away from him. "Don't."

"Why not? I know you feel the spark we've always had." He refused to give up the opportunity fate had dropped in his lap.

"Because when the sun comes up and a better offer comes your way you won't be here." Mel pushed him away and stood, her boots clomping on the floor as she glanced around in search of her clothes. She spied her tank top and grabbed it along with her bra underneath.

"I know I left you behind when I went away to college after I had promised you everything. But I'm not the same immature boy who went off to the big city. I've grown up and become the man I was meant to be. The same man who is standing here telling you that if I had one Christmas wish, if I could

73

turn back the clock, I would go back in time and tell that arrogant, horny boy to man up and hang on to you—no matter what." Then he pressed his chest against her back and gently pulled the clothing from her hands.

A small cry rushed from her as he turned her to face him, and he caught the tears that glistened on her cheeks. "I needed you and you weren't there. I know it wasn't fair. I know in my heart that you had the right to go off and live your life, but you hurt me."

His gut curdled and he wanted to rip his heart out and lay it at her feet. Two years after he'd dumped her, he went home over Christmas break to apologize, and to help her through the loss of her mother. And, to be honest, maybe see if he could repair their relationship. Instead, he'd found her in Jimmy Walsh's arms in the cab of his truck outside of her mother's trailer. He assumed she had forgotten all about him and moved on. "God, Mel."

"I waited for you for two years. Two long years of hell with a drunk mother and a two-bit job after high school that let me just get by. After she died and you didn't even show up then, I picked up the shattered pieces of my heart and moved on. A part of me will always love you, but I won't do this again. I can't." She snatched her clothes back, found the rest of them, and got dressed.

Ford recognized he had no traction with her. So he pulled himself together, grabbed his hat and coat, and started to leave. With little hope left, he went for a last ditch effort. He walked over to the bar where she had resumed cleaning, set a business card on the bar, and wrote his cell number on the back. "If you change your mind and maybe want to talk or even give us another try while I'm here through New Year's, call me. Anytime."

He moved his truck to the far corner of the lot into the deep shadows where he could watch her get safely into her car. She may not be willing to let him into her life again, but it didn't mean he stopped caring.

# Chapter Four

With her heart in her throat, Mel watched Ford leave. Damn him. Damn him for walking into her bar. Damn him for reminding her what she had missed for ten years. And damn him for making it so hard for her to stick to her plan. She hadn't expected him to say those things. To want to try again.

She threw down the bar rag, crossed her arms on the bar, and dropped her head in defeat. A single tear trickled down her cheek. Any other time of year and she would have been strong enough to walk away and never look back. But he had to come back at Christmas. Had to apologize with such sincerity that she wanted to forgive him and fly into his arms. But she couldn't do it. Couldn't trust him with her heart again.

Tears rolled down her cheeks and a sob tore from her throat. She ached for the chance to find love again, to maybe fill that gaping void in her life. Instead she let the tears fall until her throat ached and her head pounded. Then she straightened up, finished closing the bar, and went home.

In her apartment with the little Christmas tree on the table, she tried to watch TV, but couldn't get through *It's A Wonderful Life*. Instead she picked up her laptop and looked at her email. She hadn't checked it in days since she mostly got newsletters and spam mail. The first email that caught her eye made her swallow around a lump in her throat. After everything that had happened that day, of course the dating service Carla had convinced her to sign up for sent her an email.

Needing a little fortification, she got up, grabbed a beer, and headed back to her couch. She clicked on the email and waited for the message to pop up.

She skimmed through it.

*Dear Ms. Adams,*

*I am delighted to tell you that your date has been arranged for two days from now. You will arrive at The White Rose promptly at seven in the evening where a man in a black Stetson will await you. We would appreciate it if you would wear a red dress so that he may know you are the woman he is looking for. Please allow twenty-four hours' notice if you feel you cannot meet this gentleman. Enjoy, and remember to make the most of this chance.*

*Selena Markam*

*President and CEO*

*Soul Mates Dating*

Mel sipped her beer. Ill-prepared to deal with everything floating in her head, she shut the computer down. Thoughts of Ford were all tangled up in her negative feelings about her mother, and then there was her pain from his own actions. It sucked that together they had managed to ruin Christmas for her. It had always been her favorite holiday. Now it was simply a reminder that the man she loved didn't love her, and the mother who should have loved her died at the bottom of a bottle long before her body ever left the earth.

Mel turned off the lights and headed to bed. She was doing nobody any good sitting around with her depressing thoughts.

Mel stared at the card he'd left on the bar all the next day. For some reason she'd picked it up on her way out the door —she couldn't explain why, and frankly didn't want to think about it. The small white card with simple black lettering sat on her counter, taunting her.

Then she thought about her Christmas Eve date. She pulled up the email from Ms. Markam and reread it. No name was listed. How did she think Mel would know which cowboy in the black Stetson was the right one?

She looked at the card again. Should she call him? Was she crazy? People changed. She'd changed. She'd grown stronger, more self-sufficient. She hadn't had a damn choice.

The phone was in her hand before she could think about it too much. She punched in the number and let it ring. She had given up and moved to end the call, when someone picked up.

"He-whoa?" A little boy greeted her.

Her head spun and the reality that everything had changed overwhelmed her. He had a son? Her stomach heaved. She couldn't do this. Single parents were not to be trifled with. Their children should be the most important thing in their lives, and she couldn't make that kind of commitment. Not right off the bat.

"He-whoa?" The sweet voice penetrated her panic.

"I'm sorry. I have the wrong number." She disconnected the call and looked at her email again. Did she have a red dress? Hell, did she have any dress? It seemed she'd better figure it out. There was only one day left to go shopping.

Ford tried to grab the phone from Justin, but whoever called had already hung up. "Who was it, Just?"

"The lady said she had the wrong number." His nephew crushed his heart and dreams in a matter of eight words and then dashed off to go find his brothers.

Shit. His gut told him the woman had been Mel, and his nephew's voice had spooked her. He looked at the cell phone to see if her number was there. Maybe he could call her back? The last call showed an unknown number. He sighed. Guess he needed to let it go. Let her go. Not that he'd ever had any real success with doing that.

Selena had emailed him unexpectedly with a date for Christmas Eve. Apparently, she'd finally found a match for him. All the signs said he should let Mel stay in the past and move on. If she wasn't willing to try, he couldn't force her. Looked like he'd be dusting off his black Stetson for a dinner date.

Mel sat in her car and gripped the steering wheel with both hands. She could do this. She could let Ford go, push him back into the past despite his recent intrusion into her present. She grabbed her phone from the center console to climb out of the car when a wave of emotion swamped her. The horrible sense of wrongness compelled her to call him again. A kid didn't have to be a no-go for a single date. Single parents dated all the time, just look at her friend Carla.

She found the number she had dialed the day before and hit send. The phone rang and rang until voice mail picked up. Ford's warm, rich voice teased her through the receiver. He was away, blah, blah, blah. Should she leave a message? She wanted to, but the vulnerability of it, the raw exposure, scared the hell out of her. Last time it had taken two years to let go of her hope. Could she survive if this didn't work out?

She tuned back in to the message explaining how to reach him. Then he stopped talking and she expected a beep to sound. But it didn't come.

"And if this is Tuckerville, I still love you."

*Beep.*

Her heart raced as her hand trembled. She hung up the call and tried to remember back to the other night. She flipped through bits and pieces she had stored for lonely nights to come, and found the moment she was looking for. Curled up on his lap in the club chair, he'd tried to tell her how he felt as the Blake Shelton song, "Austin," filled the background. In that moment the sentiment of the song had hit way too close to home. Could she be Tuckerville? A welling of emotion told her yes. Besides, how many women could he have professed his love for in the last three days?

She couldn't go through with her date. No way, but she also couldn't leave the poor guy sitting there alone and waiting. That would be wrong. Shit. She had to walk in there and tell him tonight wasn't happening. Yes, it was past time she took responsibility for her happiness. No blaming others. No playing the victim. No excuses. She had a choice to make—and she chose Ford.

He sat at the bar of The White Rose and waited. He'd turned his phone off since every call he received had him damn near stroking out. Not to mention, he would not be rude to the woman he was meeting tonight. Even if he knew this would go nowhere and he might, as a result, miss the only call he wanted to get. A lone woman walked in—black dress. Not red. He glanced at his watch. Just past seven o'clock. He took a sip of the small batch bourbon sitting on the bar and then set the glass down while a party of ten or so came in. After a few moments, they cleared out of the foyer. As they followed the hostess into the restaurant, a woman alone by the door was revealed. She wore red. Red-hot red.

Their gazes locked across the space and his heart thundered in his chest. It couldn't be coincidence Mel stood in The White Rose wearing the very color dress he had been told to look for. Selena was a crafty witch. How had she managed this?

Ford rose as Mel sauntered over. The other night she'd been sexy as hell in a tank top, shorts, and boots. Tonight, well…tonight she was stunning. His mouth dried up like dirt at the peak of a Texas summer. His cock stood up and took notice as well, making its preference uncomfortably clear.

The red material hugged every dip and curve of her feminine form. The vee of the neckline cut low enough to entice, to tease, but not be vulgar. The slinky fabric stopped at her knees, while her legs continued on for days. His gaze landed on her trim ankles and pretty feet tucked into the sexiest pair of stilettos he'd ever seen.

"Ford?" Her soft query drew his attention back to her face.

"Hi, Mel. Fancy meeting you here." He tried for casual, but he was pretty sure he missed it by a country mile.

She blushed, a pale pink compared to her dress. "I suppose you're my date?"

He touched the brim of his hat. "If you're looking for the man in a black Stetson."

Holy hell, was she. Tight, dark denim hugged his long muscular legs and only emphasized his other endowments. Images of him sliding into her body two nights ago assailed her. She refused to look down and confirm her nipples were hard as a result.

His black shirt, boots, and blazer completed his dark and intriguing look, which challenged her ability to focus. "You used a dating service?" Damn. The words spilled out of her mouth and now she wished she could call them back. So what if he had? She'd used the same stinking service.

*Thank God I didn't leave.* The sudden thought sliced through the swirl of emotion whirling out of control inside her head.

"Why don't we have a drink, and I'll tell you how I found Soul Mate Dating." He stepped to her side and placed a possessive hand on her lower back. With his free hand he indicated the open bar stool beside the one he'd recently occupied.

"Sure." She slid on to the padded seat and the bartender approached.

"Bourbon and Diet Coke, please."

They angled toward each other and waited for her drink to be delivered. "In order to explain how I found Soul Mates, I have to tell you what happened after I broke things off." He pulled his drink toward him, caressed the curves of the glass, and traced the rim nervously. All Mel could think about was how those same strokes had felt against her skin.

"A few months after I broke it off with you I realized how stupid I was, and I dug up the gumption to go home and beg your forgiveness. I couldn't imagine you'd be willing to, but I hoped." He took a sip while the low hum of voices filled the gap in their conversation.

"I stopped in town to buy some flowers and ran into Elmer Leighton. He couldn't wait to tell me how you two had a date that night."

She practically sprayed her drink across the bar. "What? He offered to come help me with some repairs around the trailer. I was broke and desperate with Mom living in a bottle, so I accepted his offer of help. Shit, we hadn't had running water for three days. I should have been smart enough to see through his offer. It wasn't until he tried to kiss me that I figured out how naive I had been. I had to get Daddy's old shotgun to chase him off."

"Yeah. By the time I figured out he was dreaming, it was Christmas again. A whole year since I'd dumped you, so I told myself to let it go. I got so good at pretending I didn't care, I started to forget how much I actually did." He wouldn't meet her gaze, and she ached for him. "So, I hunkered down and focused on school and football. Not that it meant I could let you go. You were always on my mind. Every triumph in school or on the field had me wanting to call you."

"If only you had." Her heart hurt knowing how much they wanted each other, yet they both let foolish pride and fear stand in their way.

"If only." He lifted his gaze to lock with hers. His eyes brimmed with emotion and longing for her. "Then your mom died. I found out and drove straight back to Tuckerville, but I was too late. Too late for the funeral, and too late to be there for you. Always too late. I went straight to your trailer, but when I pulled up Jimmy's truck was parked in front and the windows were all fogged up." He shrugged. "I turned around and went back to school.

I knew then my last chance had passed me up." He tossed back another slug of bourbon.

"That was when I gave up, too. I got drunk and ended two years of celibacy. My heart kept telling me we had been good together, but my body and my head couldn't hold out any longer." He reached over and squeezed her hand sending a barrage of shivers across her skin. Her pussy softened and heated, ready for him. The man owned her, even after so long.

"Damn. I feel like an even bigger fool. But one good thing came of it all. I met Selena when we tried to date. We were both nursing broken hearts for the ones we believed were our soul mates. Of course we quickly figured out we were better as friends. So, after graduation I came into the trust fund from Grandpa Grayson. She pitched me a start-up idea for a dating service. I'd seen her ability to set people up all through college. She had a real knack for it, and I figured why not? I became a silent partner in Soul Mates Dating."

"Wow. So you...what? Saw my application—" holy crap, how pathetic had she come across in that form? "—and set up this date?"

"No. Silent partner, remember? I don't even visit the headquarters when I'm in Houston unless Selena asks me to come in, let alone review applications. No, she's been after me to let her set me up. So, I finally gave in and filled in a form of my own—a year ago." He lifted a brow to make his point.

"Wow. Shit, I keep saying that, but I'm just so surprised by all this." She reached for her drink and took her first sip. "I filled mine in a few weeks ago. One of the bartenders at The Silo sent me the link and talked me into trying it. Who could have predicted this?"

# Chapter Five

Ford might have if he'd thought about it. Somehow Selena had an almost otherworldly knack for finding other people's soul mates. Her ninety percent success rate was unparalleled in the industry. "Selena's good." He took a breath and decided to plunge ahead. "Did you happen to call yesterday and hang up as a wrong number?"

She sighed and nodded. "I did."

"Can I ask why you hung up?"

"The notion of taking on a single parent scares the hell out of me. Taking *us* on again is scary, but knowing you have a little boy who might be affected really threw me. It was so unexpected."

"*Us* scares me, too. But Justin's my nephew, and his parents are very much alive. He just beat me to my phone." It made him happy to know she had stayed there and heard him out while still believing Justin was his son.

"Oh, thank God." Her exclamation rushed out and then she blushed red enough to nearly match her dress. "I mean, don't get me wrong. I love kids. I just need some time to figure out what's happening between us before I worry about anyone else."

Ford couldn't keep the grin off his face. "So does that mean you'll give us a chance?"

She lifted her pretty blue eyes to meet his gaze and smiled. "Yes. I've missed you for so long. I'm not sure what it's like to function and not have that chronic pain, but I damn sure want to find out."

"Me, too. Do you think we could maybe get out of here?" Ford stopped and mentally cursed himself. "What I meant was, I'd really like a chance to talk somewhere more private." He gestured to the crowded bar by way of explanation.

"Talking is good. Other stuff might be better." She grinned at him. "Besides, my roommate is out all night." She slid off the barstool and ran her hands over her hips.

Ford's mouth dried up again. He quickly paid their tab, gathered their coats, and led her outside. She gave him her address and then he tried his damnedest to keep up with her. Some things sure hadn't changed. Mel was still a speed demon behind the wheel.

Ford parked near her and they walked into the building together. Her apartment was on the fifth floor and had a nice view of Austin, but all she really wanted was to see Ford Grayson naked. She locked the door behind them and turned to find him staring out the window.

"So, Ford, how would *us* work since I assume you still live in Tuckerville and run your parents' ranch—well, your ranch. I have a good job here, but it doesn't exactly lend itself to flexibility." She walked over to the fridge and pulled out a bottle. "Beer?"

"Thanks." He took the cold bottle from her. "I suppose I can try to spend most weekends here and leave my foreman in charge. He's a good man and I trust him to get things done without me there. Or, if weekends are too busy, I can cut out a few days a week here and there. I guess we'll have to work it out as we go."

He took a long pull on the bottle, his neck muscles working to pull the beverage down. Something about watching him swallow like that was damn sexy. "Okay. I'll see if I can finagle the schedule a bit better so I can have a weekend off every now and then to come to your place. I've been meaning to start training Carla as an assistant manager. Guess I should get on that." She grinned.

He lowered the bottle and met her gaze. "Guess you'd better." He set the bottle down and crooked his finger at her. "Come here, Mel."

She bit her lip and walked toward him. Not normally a submissive woman, she loved the look of pure power in his eyes when she did his bidding.

He pulled her into his arms and dropped his lips onto hers. He plundered her mouth, slowly stroking between her lips to taste every corner and crevice. She swore he mapped the inside of her mouth. He ran his tongue across her teeth, probed beneath her tongue, and tangled with hers in a sexy and naughty promise of what would come. His mouth was cool and faintly sweet from the light beer he'd just sucked down.

His hands wandered from her waist to her hips and then down to her bottom. He grabbed a fistful of cheek in each hand and pulled her flush against him. Finally the need to breathe overrode the need to taste him, and she pulled back.

"God, I don't remember you being able to make me forget everything with a kiss. I think I like the older, more experienced Ford."

"Well, while you were always a hot little thing, I don't remember you requiring a sign that warned of dangerous curves. You shaped up real nice, Mel." He leaned down and kissed her again.

With a whimper of desire, she clung to his broad shoulders and let him ravage her mouth. She stroked and tasted with as much fervor as he did, but if she let go of his shoulders she would crumple in a heap of jellied limbs. He broke the kiss and tried to put some space between them. "We need to talk about a few things."

She leaned in to rekindle their kiss, but he placed his fingers over her lips and stopped her.

"I'm serious, Mel. We need to talk." The man groaned. Then he swept her up into his arms and carried her to the couch, and sat down with her straddled across his legs. The slinky red dress rode up on her thighs to reveal her sexy matching garters.

"No, we don't. Not right now. Not when I need you to fill me with your cock." She shifted so that her thighs pressed against the outer edges of his and drew his gaze south to the black lace bands held up by red clips.

He groaned and shut his eyes. "Mel, I'm trying to do the right thing here. Please…"

He sounded so pained, so determined that as much as she wanted to snatch open his pants and climb on his pole, she didn't. And that was some Xena-like restraint. She slid off his lap, straightened her dress, and settled next to him.

"Okay. Talk."

He clenched his hands into fists as he shifted so they faced each other. "We didn't use a condom last time. Are you okay with that or do I need to glove up?"

"We're good. I trust you and like I said, I'm on the pill."

"All right. The things we did last time, when I tied you up. If we're gonna keep playing like that, we need some ground rules to keep us both safe."

"Ford, you aren't the first guy that's tied me up." Her cheeks heated. She did not want to talk with him about this stuff. About her past.

A small muscle in his jaw leapt at her statement. Then it continued to tick in a steady rhythm that drew her attention. "Everything we do has to be safe, sane, and consensual. What we did the other night is only the tip of my iceberg. I'm not the same boy you knew. I have a darker side, a more dominant side than you remember."

He was right, she didn't know him. Not really. Damn it, once again she dove headfirst into Ford's end of the swimming hole. Last time she did that he left her treading water alone. The cool air teased her lace-covered nipples and skated across her flesh. "You're right. I don't really know Ford the man, but I want to." She remained still on the couch, while hope burned in her chest. The wait didn't last long. Seized by big strong hands and hauled into his lap, he settled her against his chest.

"I'm not trying to scare you, Mel, but I don't want you to look back on this and regret what we did. Regret giving us a chance, even if it doesn't work out."

She drew a breath and leaned away from his warmth. Some things never changed. Ford remained her knight, her protector. His armor was dirty and dented, it no longer shone. But, at his core, he was the same person she had loved since high school. She placed her palms against each of his cheeks and forced him to look her in the eyes. "The only regret I have right now is that I let you walk away without a fight. The other night was so unexpected and so damn hot my panties have been wet ever since. I couldn't regret a single thing about giving us a second chance, and for the record you don't scare me."

But loving him? That scared the crap out of her. Pushing aside her racing heart, she pressed her lips to his and pushed her tongue into his mouth. She punctuated her statement with a demanding kiss that explored and teased even as pleasure zinged from her lips to her toes.

He growled as he tore his mouth from hers. In one swift move, he flipped her onto her back and pinned her arms over her head. His breath sawed in and out of his lungs in desire-fueled gulps and told her how affected he was. "I need to know what your boundaries are, that you are participating because you want to, not because I made you, and I need to know that you understand how to bring things to a halt. I need to know these things because, Mel, I am going to test every boundary you set. I am going to butt up against them and maybe bust a few, and in the end I am going to make you scream with pleasure until you pass out from exhaustion."

Her hips bucked reflexively against his hips as he straddled her on the couch. With her arms pinned, all she could do was talk. There was no distracting him. No using her body to draw his attention where she wanted it. "God, Ford. Please. Please make me scream." She closed her eyes and focused on trying to rub against the hard ridge of his erection.

"Limits, Mel." The command in his voice seared through her lust soaked haze and grabbed her attention.

"I-I d-don't know. The ropes were good." She glanced around unable to fully focus to find the words to say what she wanted. This side of Ford was familiar from the other night, yet new. He was much more intense. More demanding. Just...more.

"Spanking?" He snapped out the question.

"God, yes."

"Anal?"

"Yes."

"Coming on you?" He ground his cock against her pussy.

"Mmmmm..." Mel let her eyes close as she imagined him standing over her and shooting his—

Smack. Her thigh tingled where he slapped her.

"Focus, darlin'. Right here, eyes on me."

She stared into his eyes and waited.

"Coming on you was a yes. Light pain?"

"Some. No whips. Nothing crazy. Pinch my nipples, stuff like that."

"Okay, what's your safe word?" He kept her wrists pinned with one hand and used his free fingers to trace over her lips and each cheekbone.

"Uncle."

"Uncle it is. You understand if you use it, everything stops then and there."

"Yes…" Her lids drifted down and blocked out the sight of him looming over her. "Do I call you something? Sir or master, or something?"

"No titles. Just be respectful." He kissed her left eye lid. "Responsive." He did the same on the right. "Honest." He kissed her lips with a gentle sweep of his. "And true to yourself. If something I want or suggest doesn't work for you, then I expect you to use your safe word tonight."

"I will." She pressed up against his heat.

"And, darlin', we will do a thorough formal agreement on limits real soon. Now, I want you to stand up and strip for me."

She nodded and he released her wrists. Standing on rubbery legs, she peeled off her sexy red armor to reveal her black and red lingerie.

"All of it." Ford sat back against the couch and willed himself not to leap on her as she unveiled the rest of her flesh for him. Damn, he couldn't wait to sink back into her hot, tight pussy. Then she turned around and bent over to pull her panties down. Her shaved, pink pussy peeked out at him. The light glistened off the wet folds and beckoned him to take action. He leaned forward, placed one hand on each of her upper thighs, and said, "Don't move."

Her legs quivered beneath his touch, even as he pressed forward and dipped his tongue into her juices. He traced the moisture-soaked slit from between her thighs to her seeping channel. Her breath hitched as his dick throbbed. "Ford?"

"Yeah, Mel?" His response rumbled in his chest as he clenched her thighs tighter.

"Fuck me. Please?" Her whimpered request pushed him past all his good intentions of pleasuring her before filling her.

Good intentions would have to wait for next time. "Grab your ankles, darlin'." He stood up, practically ripped his pants open, and in a single stroke plunged deep into her waiting depths. Oh God, she was everything he remembered and more. Her pussy clenched his shaft in a choke hold that had his hips bucking involuntarily. Deeper. More.

"Oh..." She drew the one word out on a sigh.

Ford slid backwards until only the tip was lodged in her opening and then he shoved back in. He retreated again, a little quicker this time, and then sank deep inside her. As his pace increased, her gasps and sexy little noises amplified. Within a few minutes, he pounded into her as though his life depended on how thoroughly he fucked her.

As deep as he was, it was not enough. He needed to be so far inside her that he couldn't crawl out for days, years, maybe ever. Yeah, forever sounded real good right at that moment. He thrust into her, his hands gripping her hips and pulling her backwards with every thrust forward as she held on to her ankles.

Trust. She trusted him to keep her safe. Trusted him, despite all the other times he'd failed her, to take care of her. Trusted him to see to her pleasure.

He reached around and burrowed between her thighs to find her clit. When he found the slick nub, swollen to the size of a pea, he stroked it. She shattered around him in a breathtaking orgasm that hurtled him over the edge right behind her. With a mindless shout of pleasure he slammed his cock into her over and over as he filled her with his cum.

*Mine.*

It was an animalistic thought ripped from his guts. He'd always known it, even when he was denying the truth. There could be no other woman for him. Ever.

As they tumbled back to reality, he collapsed back onto the couch and pulled her with him. Still joined, he clutched her to his chest. "You're mine, Mel. I'll never give you up again."

She stilled in his arms, slipped off his softening dick and then off his lap. She turned to face him, knelt between his thighs, and got right in his face. "You can't give up what won't go away. If you ever get stupid on me again, I guarantee I will tie you to the bed until you come to your senses. I swear to you I will use every weapon at my disposal to make you see the error of your ways. I love you, Ford. I always have, and God help me I always will."

"I love you, too, darlin'." Then he scooped her up and kissed her while he prayed to any God who'd listen to let him keep her.

At some point, they parted to allow air into their oxygen starved lungs. She smiled that sexy, taunting little smile he remembered from high school. She pulled it out whenever she was angling to get him to do something, and it usually involved challenging him in some way.

"Now that we broke the ice, how about you try finding some of those boundaries of mine you claimed you were gonna butt up against."

"Careful what you wish for..." He arched a brow and stared at the vixen who'd fulfilled every Christmas wish he'd made since his freshman year of college. "You just might get it, I sure did. Merry Christmas, darlin'."

The End

# Roping His Cowboy

*One Night With A Cowboy*
Book 4
**Sorcha Mowbray**

# Chapter One

"Four years, Shane. Four years of shooting for a national championship and the closest we've come is getting eliminated in the first round of nationals three years ago. I don't wanna live on the road forever, man." *Except it's the one way livin' with you makes sense.*

"I hear ya'. I'm tired, too."

Silence hung thick in the ratty motel room as they each carried a sweat coated bottle of beer to their lips and pulled a long swig. Brig cut a glance to his right and watched as his best friend's esophagus worked to pull the cold liquid down his throat. He repressed a groan as an image of the familiar face tipped up at exactly the same angle swept in but this time he fed his cock down his throat. Shit. The raunchy, sexy images were popping into his head more and more frequently. To the point he hadn't laid a hand on a buckle bunny in over a year.

Despite the fact Shane never ogled girls with the rest of the guys—he'd always chalked it up to his gentlemanly nature—he never would've pegged his roping partner as gay. Then one afternoon his economics class let out early and he decided to see if Shane wanted to get some extra practice in. He had a key to Shane's apartment since he often flopped there between classes. The place had been quiet, but the familiar old red pickup sat in the driveway so his teammate should have been home. He'd wandered back toward his room and gently nudged the cracked door open.

To his shock, he found a fully clothed Shane on his knees swallowing a solid seven inches of long hard cock as he made happy slurping noises punctuated by Johnny's low growls. The dark haired guy's words rang in his head.

"That's it, Shane. Take it all, like you always do." He reached down to fist his hand in the blond mop of hair and pumped his hips into Shane's face. "Suck it good, man."

He'd spun around and bolted from the scene unsure what to say or do. It wasn't that he had a problem with his buddy being gay, it was that he'd never said anything. And there was the small issue of the hard on he ignored as he fled the scene.

A few months later, drunk, horny and alone Brig found himself jerking off to the memory. After graduation they'd gone on the road together. Sometime during the first year he started replacing Johnny with himself. Imagined how it would feel to shove his own cock down his best friend's throat and fuck it like he never could with the girls he'd been with. The fantasy grew over the years until after he pumped his load down Shane's throat he pulled him up, spun him around and fucked him in the ass with a dick that never flagged. Because, deny it all he might, something about that golden boy really flipped his switch.

Except he wasn't gay. He liked women. He found them sexy and soft and… different.

"Hey, maybe we should sign up for a dating service? One of my friends gave me the name of this site that seems to have a seriously uncanny ability to match people with their perfect partner."

*But I've found mine.* Where the hell had that thought come from? "Dating service? I don't know man."

Shane shrugged and focused his dark brown gaze on him. "Couldn't hurt could it? Come on. Just for shits and giggles. Fill in the questionnaire."

Silence.

"You don't even have to show it to me. Just do it and send one in."

Three beers in Brig found his resistance to the ridiculous idea crumbling. "Fine. What's the site?"

"Soulmatesdating.com. And be honest or it won't work. My friend said the more honest you are the more likely it is to work." Shane grinned and Brig found his stomach doing an all too familiar slow roll.

God, when had he fallen for another guy? How had it happened? He pulled up the website on his laptop and started filling in the questions. A glance over at Shane showed him frowning in concentration at his computer. With a shrug, he looked back at his screen. First question: Do you prefer women or men? A familiar voice in his head urged, be honest. He typed one word.

Either.

His gut twisted, but it seemed a weight lifted. He suspected he wasn't really into men as much as he was into Shane, but he'd seen a man or two over the years who struck him as attractive in a sexual way. Not many. But one or two. And then there was his best friend and the star of all his porny fantasies. He was all man and he definitely turned him on. Focus. Fill in the rest of the questions. And when he hit send a small spark of hope ignited in his chest.

Six months later...

Shane's heart pounded in his chest as the saddle creaked with each restless shift of his horse, Smoke. On the other side of the chute Brig sat calmly astride Thor. All around them the crowd rumbled with subdued anticipation. This was the Justin Boots Playoffs championship round for Team Roping. If they won here they would seal a spot at the National Finals Rodeo—the NFR.

This was a big event. Pushing aside the distracting thoughts he listened as the announcer introduced them.

"Next up is header John Brigham paired with heeler Shane Goodson. These two have been burning up the standings on their way to the NFR in Vegas."

*No pressure.* Shane snorted. His best friend in the world stared into his eyes, and he stared back. He gave a thumbs-up and then Brig nodded. The steer shot down the chute between them and they took off after the target. The steer cleared the chute clean with the hunky header right on his tail. Rope high he followed only slightly behind. Then Brig hooked the horns and turned the beast so he could cut the corner and snare the heels. Their horses faced each other, ropes drawn tight stretching the back end of the animal between them for a moment. Just long enough to stop the clock at 4.5 seconds.

Their time put them at the top of the leader board. With two more teams to go in the final round they'd know soon if they won.

They exited the arena and quickly returned to the area behind the chutes so they could watch the remaining teams. Brig climbed up next to him on the rail. "Nice job. That ought'a cinch it for us."

"Damn it. Don't jinx us."

Chaz and Dean, their biggest competition, went next. The header, Chaz, shot out and snagged the horns clean, but the steer wrestled a bit and tried to go heavy to avoid the second rope. He had to fight a bit to get him turned clean so Dean could catch the heels. By the time they stretched the cattle the clock showed 5.10 seconds.

"Well folks, that leaves these boys in second place for now," the announcer confirmed.

The last team was introduced and then the steer started down the chute. But something went wrong as the header turned the animal the heeler cut in too close and couldn't catch the feet right.

No score.

Brig wrapped his beefy arms around him and for a moment Shane knew heaven. He inhaled the scent of man, horse, leather, and a trace of soap. So fucking sexy.

*Baseball, laundry, pot roast...*

Down. He needed his boner to go down. Now. Preferably before his best friend figured out how badly he wanted him. Then he let go and turned to accept congratulations from the circle of well-wishers surrounding them. They'd done it. They were headed back to the NFR.

Two blocks from their motel was The Rusty Nail. It was a local honky-tonk where most of the rodeo cowboys hung out when they were in town. Largely because it was stumbling distance to their beds. Brig sucked back another beer glad neither he nor Shane had to worry about getting home beyond who was gonna lean on who while they walked back to the room.

For maybe the tenth time that night he sent another wannabe rodeo queen packing. Tonight was about him and Shane. His friend pulled up beside him at the bar and grabbed his beer. "Saw another sad-eyed cowgirl pass as I came back. Turned her down, too?"

Did he think it was strange he hadn't claimed one of the many girls offering

94

to be his trophy tonight? He hadn't bothered in so long he didn't think it would seem strange anymore. "Not my type."

"Long hair, red lips, tits, ass, willing. What about that combo ain't your type?" The sexy blond cowboy's eyebrows would have pushed his hat off if they got any higher.

"Over processed. Too sparkly. Not my thing." Brig shrugged and swallowed more beer. *Please, let this go.*

"Damn. I'm impressed. I figured you were holding off, focusing on the Finals. But since we're in, I guess I figured you'd break this celibate streak."

"Ain't about that." *It's about you.* God, how he wanted to tell him the truth. But the big tough cowboy was too scared to tell his friend how he felt. To tell him the truth about who starred in all his jerk-off material.

"Huh." Shane tipped up his beer and swallowed the last of the golden liquid. "Well, I think I've had enough celebrating for one night. I'm gonna head back."

"Yeah? We probably should call it a night. Got a long drive tomorrow to Oregon."

Together they left and started down the street to their motel. Shane yammered on about the other teams they would be up against at the Finals. Man, he loved breaking down the competition and seeing where they needed to improve to stay competitive. Then he changed topics as they hit the parking lot of the dump they called home for the night. "So you remember Johnny, my old roommate?"

The name came out the dark like a sucker punch to the gut. He stumbled. "Johnny?"

"Yeah. You okay man? I didn't think you had so much to drink you couldn't walk." Shane's big expressive brown eyes filled with worry.

"I'm fine. Just hit a big rock. So what'd he want?" He tried not to growl the last part, but it was a near thing. Shane rarely talked about the guy after he suddenly moved out their senior year of college. They showed up after class one day to find all his stuff gone. No note. Nothing. He had moved in with Shane after that.

"Nothing really, just wanted to see how I was doing. Guess he came across an article about us and he decided to look me up." Something almost vulnerable crept into his voice.

"He say anything about that disappearing act he pulled?"

They unlocked the door to their room and stepped in. Shane shut the door and locked it behind them. "Yeah. He apologized for lighting out like that."

"That's it? No explanation?" Brig wanted to punch the jerk in the face. He'd always assumed it had been some lover's quarrel but obviously Shane wasn't gonna tell him that since he wasn't supposed to know he was gay.

"You know, some things came up unexpectedly. He had to roll." Shane seemed to shut down after that.

Silence stretched taught between them and Brig considered telling him he knew he was gay, but it seemed like such an invasion of privacy. And, if he was honest with himself, it still stung that after all these years of being friends there wasn't enough trust for Shane to come out.

They stripped down to their boxers and Shane disappeared into the bathroom. He decided to get a glass of water from the sink and had just set the empty glass down when the man of his fantasies stepped out of the bathroom and into his arms.

"Whoa. Sorry, man." Brig moved to step back but Shane refused to let him go.

Hands trembling, Shane slid them from his shoulders up to his stubble dusted face. Confusion and need darkened his brown eyes even as he closed the distance between them. Brig ached to chase away the sadness in his partner's eyes, but knew he would never make a move. Too damned scared.

"I'm not," Shane muttered and leaned in to plant his lips on Brig's.

Full, firm masculine lips claimed his sending a bolt of surprise through his body to make his cock stand up at attention. Shane's tongue flicked out to trace the inside of his mouth. And then, with a needy groan he turned his head and deepened the kiss. Taking in the musky flavor of man mixed with the light crisp taste of beer caused a moment of panic laced desire to surge through him. Then Shane's hands gripped his waist as they pressed closer together. Hard cocks rubbed creating mind blowing friction that made his knees tremble. And when he started kissing Shane back? Brig damn near blew his wad right there.

Then he realized he was kissing Shane. No fantasy. All real, all the time. And the panic took over.

He pushed his walking wet dream away and said what he believed he should. What a straight guy should when another man came on to him. "What the fuck, dude?"

His best friend paled and stepped away. "You wanted it as much as I did." But shame lowered his eyes and he refused to look at him.

"No way." Shit. He knew. With unnecessary force he pushed past his stunned friend and got in the queen bed he claimed earlier for his own. Desperate to hide the truth in the shadows he turned off the lamp. "Just go to sleep. Clearly you had too much to drink."

A low growl of anger rumbled from the darkness by the sink. Then Shane navigated through the dark until he found the other bed with his shins and cursed softly. Brig lay in bed and pretended to sleep as he listened to his friend toss and turn at one point, deep in the night he swore he heard a sniffle but refused to acknowledge how cruel he'd been.

Finally near dawn he drifted into a fitful sleep.

# Chapter Two

Shane rolled out of bed shortly after the first rays of sunshine peeked through the threadbare drapes of the motel room. The room where he laid it all on the line in a moment of drunken vulnerability and had his dreams crushed. He'd dreamed of tasting Brig's kiss since the first day he laid eyes on him in college. But as a gay man in the west, let alone the rodeo community, he knew better than to believe he had the option to be open about his preferences. His parents knew and supported him no matter his choices, but they agreed he was smart to keep things quiet.

Eyes gritty with a lack of sleep he shuffled to the bathroom to take care of nature and will the blue balls from the night before to stop aching. A pit formed in his stomach when he heard Brig get up and move around. How awkward could this be? He drew a deep breath and stepped out.

"Morning." Brig shuffled by him and into the bathroom.

Okay, at least he offered his normal surly greeting. He'd never been a morning person.

By the time he dressed Brig came out and went about donning his own clothes. "I'll go grab us some coffee and breakfast."

"Sounds good."

An hour later as their truck chewed up blacktop, horse trailer behind them, they kept to their sides of the big quad cab. But then they always sought space while driving. *How can he pretend nothing happened?* It rankled a bit their lip lock hadn't caused more of a stir with Brig.

Two hours later and Shane passed annoyed headed straight for pissed off. "You gonna stop soon?"

"Nope." He didn't even look over.

He huffed. "You planning on being silent the entire drive to Redmond?"

"Didn't realize I was being quiet. Wonder who else will be competing at Redmond?" Brig spit a wad of sunflower seeds into a cup and set it back in the cup holder by the gearshift.

"I don't know." Shane wanted to pout like a child, but tried to rein in the urge.

"Really? You're usually pretty up on who will be where."

Shane refused to respond. What was he supposed to say? Sorry I was too busy worrying what my straight roping partner thought of the very gay kiss I laid on him last night.

Endless pavement stretched out before them and behind them. Another forty minutes passed and with each mile his anger at being tossed aside boiled hotter and hotter. The silence had grown so thick you needed a cleaver to slice through it, and then Shane's patience snapped. "So this is it? We're just gonna pretend that kiss last night didn't happen?"

"I don't know what you're talking about." Brig's grip on the steering wheel tightened until his knuckles turned white.

"Last night. When I kissed you. When I had my tongue so far down your throat I could have confirmed you no longer have tonsils." Anger and indignation pushed him to lash out at his friend.

"Must have been some drunken dream you had there." Brig snorted and then turned the radio on letting the latest country tune blast through the cab.

Frustrated, angry, and more than a little hurt, Shane dropped the subject but the pot continued to boil. When they finally pulled in to the rodeo grounds he hopped out of the truck and slammed the door closed before Brig had even moved. He had the horse trailer opened and was leading Smoke down the ramp when Brig came around. The dark haired, green eyed devil stood there hands shoved in his pockets. Did he want to say something? Anything? Shane's heart pounded with hope and anticipation.

He cleared his throat and it sounded like a rusty bucket of nails churning. "Man, look I…"

"Hey, guys." Chaz Markham pulled up by the corrals and climbed out of his rig. "Long drive, huh?"

Brig flushed and turned away. "Yeah, it was."

Damn it. Shane wanted to punch the flashy dickhead in the mouth. Chaz and his partner Dean had won the NFR Team Roping event two years running and he liked to remind everyone of that fact. "Figured you two would be off resting up now that you're finally back in the Finals."

"Why is that?" Shane led his horse off the ramp and headed for the corral gate.

Chaz grinned and opened up his trailer. "Well, you know I figured after you two burned out a few years ago you'd take any advantage you could get to try and beat me and Dean. So, you know resting up seemed like a smart move."

Shane snorted and ignored the bait. Brig, not so much. "Yeah, cause we're so old. Right?"

"You feeling old?" Chaz smirked.

"God, twenty-two and you think you have it all figured out. Have fun finding out what it's like to have life throw you on your ass."

"Don't be mad that we've had more success than you guys." The blond kid poked the bear.

"Don't fool yourself. One day, maybe sooner than you think, rodeoin' won't be an option. I sure hope you did more with your winnings than blow it on a fancy rig and fancy boots." He pointed at the shiny trailer and super pointy boots with silver tips.

Brig had just closed the gate behind Thor when Chaz snarled, "No man, I spent plenty on your sister to say thanks for the ride."

Brig roared and threw his fist into the perfectly sculpted face attached to Chaz. Bone crunched against bone as he made contact. The smart mouthed punk hit the dirt and yelled as he grabbed his face. Blood spurted everywhere as people from all around them came running to see what the ruckus was.

"What the hell man?" Chaz cried from the ground like he hadn't been provoking Brig only a moment before.

Shane cursed and grabbed Brig's arm, "Let's go man. That brat is just gonna make more trouble if we stick around."

Brig nodded and climbed into the passenger side after Shane redirected him. Whether he knew it or not, his roping hand was hurt. They pulled away from the grounds and found the motel pretty quick. After checking in Shane sent Brig to the room as he pulled their gear out and brought it to the room. The angry hulk of a man sat on one of the beds with his hand submerged in a bucket of ice and water.

Shane tossed everything on the other bed and stalked over to him. "You shouldn't let that little shit rile you up like that."

"Hell. I know, but he's so damn cocksure. Makes me want to knock him on his ass." He looked up with wary eyes.

He couldn't help but smile at him. "Well, you sure did that."

Brig flashed a grin before he went back to brooding.

He reached for his hand in the bucket, "Let me take a look."

"I'm good."

"Just let me see how bad it is." He grabbed for the hand and Brig whipped it out of the bucket which caused the lightweight container to tumble from his lap and spill all over his thighs and the bedspread.

"Goddamn it, Shane!" He jumped up and knocked him over onto the other bed. "Don't touch me." He shoved past him over to the vanity area.

"Fuck you." Shane leapt up and followed him as he pushed him up against the wall. "Why shouldn't I touch you?"

Breath sawed in and out of his lungs from the adrenalin rush of having Shane touch him or maybe it was just fear, either way resulted in the same thing. Light headed and still angry about his reaction to Chaz he swung at his best friend.

Shane blocked the feeble blow and pinned his arms against the wall. "Goddamn you, Brig. I will not hit you. Not even after the way you treated me last night."

Hurt and anger simmered in those big dark pools of chocolate. Made him feel ashamed for how he'd acted the night before and again now. "Shit." He let his head tip back against the wall.

"How long have you known?" Shane let go of his arms and stepped back.

He pushed up from the wall and moved by the sink where he ran some cold

101

water and rinsed his hand for a minute. When the throbbing eased again he turned it off, but he still hadn't decided where to start. "Since our junior year of college."

"Well, shit." The sexy blonde cowboy flopped on the dry bed next to their bags and let his arm drape over his face. "Why didn't you say anything?"

Pain, not the physical kind, seared through him. "Why didn't you? I thought we were best friends."

"You're still a cowboy. It's just not something you say to another guy in our world. Not unless you know how he'll react. How'd you find out?"

He brushed off the stereotype comment. "I walked in on you sucking Johnny off one day. Left without saying anything. I figured you'd tell me if you wanted me to know."

"That must have been a shock."

"You're telling me." Brig remained by the vanity, but leaned against it. "Were you two lovers?"

Shane snorted and moved his arm. "No. He was a straight guy who discovered nobody gives head as well as another guy. He used me until the day his girlfriend walked in on us." A bitter laugh escaped him. "Guess she wasn't the only one to find us like that."

"Nope." Brig pushed off the counter and walked toward his friend. "Don't sweat it man."

Shane sat up. "What the hell does that mean?"

"Who you prefer to do in the bedroom doesn't change things with us." He started to walk away but Shane rose up and blocked him. "The hell it doesn't. Your dick got as hard as mine last night when we kissed. Admit it."

"Let it go, man." Brig made to brush past him but Shane shoved his chest up against the wall and grabbed his uninjured arm. With a quick twist and a strong grip forged by years of heeling and ranching his best friend pinned him face first against the wall.

"Admit it, damn you. Admit you liked my hands on you, my mouth." Shane's demand sent shivers of awareness down Brig's spine to lodge in his balls and radiate up his shaft.

"No." He grit the denial out for fear if he admitted the truth all hell would break loose and he would tackle Shane so he could fuck him into the mattress. His control hung by a thread.

Shane grunted and then he brought Brig's other hand around to meet the one behind his back. Next he knew, his friend had him tied up and unable to move his arms.

"What the fuck are you doing?" Anger surged to the fore and he knew if his arms weren't tied he'd be swinging at Shane again for this shit.

"Apparently you need a lesson in how to be honest. Because right now you are lying to me and yourself." He turned him around, pushed him up against the wall and unfastened his buckle.

Then the button and zipper on his jeans slid past his iron hard dick. Hard to deny the truth when everything about Shane, from his golden hair to his rock hard body, turned him on and it was obvious. His heart nearly stopped as his fantasy came to life and dropped to his knees before him. *Aw fuck.* He tugged his jeans and boxers down around his knees and then leaned forward to nuzzle his cock.

"Holy shit you smell as good as I imagined you would." Then Shane whipped his tongue out and dragged it over Brig's ball sac and up the length of his cock.

"Fuck." Brig couldn't believe what happened. Had never expected to know the pleasure of Shane's mouth on his cock, but here he was watching the sexy as hell cowboy lap at his dick. Cupping his balls with one hand, he used the other to grip the base while he flicked his tongue over the glistening tip again and again. Then he opened his mouth and popped the tip in to suck it like a hard candy treat.

Brig's legs shook as he used his bound hands and shoulders to brace against the only solid thing in the room, the wall. With a mischievous grin Shane swallowed more of his length and he swore he'd never seen anything so fucking hot as watching inch after inch of his dick disappear into that kissable, fuckable mouth. When he didn't think any more would fit his fantasy man swallowed and his tip slid past the muscle of his throat and deep inside. "Oh, fuck." It was all he could manage as that blond head bobbed up and down on his dick fucking him good while he squeezed his sac with the perfect amount of pressure to prolong the ecstasy.

Spit dribbled down his balls and over his fingers as they worked him until he let go and one of those spit soaked fingers pressed against his pucker. He tensed up at first, but the finger kept massaging the nerves back their gently urging him to relax. All the while that hot wet mouth pulsed around his cock creating the most incredible sensations. As he focused on how good it all felt he opened and that finger slid deep in his ass. An initial feeling of weirdness drew him up short, but then as Shane's digit pushed further he discovered just how good it could be. Inside him Shane stroked his prostate as he increased the suction on his cock. Brig groaned and his hips jerked forward and stroked into that welcoming mouth only to pull out and impale himself on the long thick finger buried in his anal passage. Together they found a rhythm that suited Brig's need to be in control—even while his hands were bound behind him. He looked down and saw his darkest dreams come to life with Shane's lips wrapped around his cock. He'd never included the finger, but that was due to lack of knowledge. Had he known? Yeah, that finger would have been right where it was. In fact. "Add another finger. More."

Shane groaned around his cock as he jammed a second digit in with the first and Brig's head exploded. All the blood rushed from his big head to his cock and he cried out, "Oh shit. Gonna come."

He tried to push Shane off his cock, unsure if he would want to swallow his load, but the choice proved not to be his. Shane stayed rooted in place as he madly pumped those fingers in and out of Brig's ass until his knees shook and stars dotted his vision. "Fuck!" Hot cream gushed from his cock as he sprayed the back of Shane's throat. Greedy for every drop Shane refused to release his cock as he gulped as much as he could. When Brig thought no more would come out his sexy friend let him slip out until the head remained in his mouth and continued to suck the last drops from his dick.

Shane let his forehead drop against his thigh as they both tried to gather their composure. Without a word, Shane released his bonds, rose up, and left the room.

Stunned by what had happened and the sudden flight of his friend he tripped over the jeans bunched around his ankles and fell. By the time he got his clothes hauled up and fastened he caught Shane climbing into their truck.

# Chapter Three

Fuck. *What'd I do?* Shane strode toward their truck, half hoping Brig would chase him down. The other half feared what might happen if he did. Would he try to punch him in the face like he had Chaz? *What a fucking mess.* Not only had he blown their friendship but also the best roping partner he could have hoped for.

He swung the door of the truck open but never made it inside. A big, familiar, hand landed on his shoulder and spun him around. Before he could say a word or get his hands up to protect his face Brig came at him. He shoved him up against the side of the vehicle and then they were pressed body to body as Brig's kissable lips slammed against his in a tooth grinding claiming that shook Shane right down to his toes.

As they clung to each other, tongues tangled, everything around them fell away. Nothing else mattered but the bone deep awareness of the man in his arms and the overpowering emotion swelling from the depths of his soul.

Brig drew back, breath heaving in and out of his chest. "Come back to the room."

Breath stolen by the most amazing kiss, Shane nodded and followed the man who dominated his every thought whether he wanted it or not. He closed the door as Brig sat on one of the beds.

"You're right." Color dusted his already tanned cheeks. "I like your hands on me. Been thinking about nothing but that and more since I walked in on you with your roommate in college."

"Christ Brig. We've been out of school for four years." His heart pounded with hope and adrenalin.

"Yeah, well it's taken me a little time to get used to the idea."

"Am I so hard to…" He couldn't say the word.

"Shit Shane. I've always been attracted to women. Never once thought about a guy in a sexual way until I walked in on you sucking Johnny's cock. I'd never seen anything like it and so help me, I was jealous of him. I wanted it to be my cock in your mouth, my fist in your hair."

He sat down on the bed across from his best friend, the man he'd desired since the moment he laid eyes on him at the University of Wyoming Rodeo Team's first meeting of the school year. Too bad he fell in love about five minutes after that when Brig smiled and introduced himself as he sat down. "I always imagined it was you I was blowing. Wanted it to be you, but you were straight and you never let on otherwise."

"You were right, back then. But I've come to accept maybe I'm bi or whatever. I don't know what you call it. But when it comes to you, the only label I can use is love."

Holy crap.

Before Shane could respond, Brig launched himself across the two feet separating them and knocked him to the bed. "Say something, man."

A shiver rolled through him as one hundred and eighty pounds of muscular man pinned him to the mattress and declared his love. "God, I love you. I've loved you for so long." Then he reached up, sifted his fingers through Brig's slightly shaggy dark hair, and yanked him down into a kiss. Less violent than the one by the truck, but no less powerful. He drove past lips and teeth to slip his tongue over his inner landscape. He tasted man, a little mint from the gum he'd chewed earlier, and desire. Fuck he tasted like pure desire.

Brig reached between them and cupped his dick through the confining denim. He pumped his hips in answer to the silent question. Yes, fuck yes. He shifted his hand up and unfastened Shane's belt followed by the button and fly of his jeans. Then he broke the kiss, slithered the length of his body, and landed on the floor between his legs. Gaze bright with the years of friendship and freshly exposed love he reached up and jerked his jeans down his legs along with his boxers.

Brig couldn't believe this was happening. A growl escaped as he leaned in and swiped the length of his cock with his tongue. Long, thick, and hard as steel, reality far exceeded his imagination. The tip glistened as pre-come dribbled out to creep down the head. Taking a moment to savor the image, to revel in the knowledge all that hardness was for him. No longer able to resist, he swirled around the head and let the salty taste roll over his tongue. Then he popped the whole thing in his mouth and inched his way down the rigid length. Shane moaned and gripped his head tighter as he swallowed all of him. Well, as much of him as he could take. Clearly taking all of him would take some practice.

"Oh, fuck, Brig."

The words drew him back to the man on the bed under his control. Yeah, he fucking loved that. He continued to suck until Shane's hips bucked up with each down-stroke. He released his dick and rose up. "I wanna fuck you. Wanna sink into your tight ass until I'm balls deep and then I'm gonna fuck you until there is no question in your mind that you belong to me."

"Damn, man. How'd you hide this from me for so long?" Shane got up, grabbed the hem of Brig's shirt, and yanked up until the material blocked his view. Then the material disappeared and the hot cowboy in front of him had on way too much clothing.

"Don't know. Don't care. Not hiding anymore." He unbuckled his belt and kicked off his boots. "Shirt off."

Shane didn't say a word as he ripped his own shirt off over his head, ditched his boots and the jeans bunched around his ankles.

Brig walked over to his friend's bag and pulled out the tube of lube he knew was there.

"How'd you know I had that?"

"You never really hid it. I never said anything." He sauntered back toward the bed, lust pushing him to discover everything he'd imagined while love urged him to be careful with the man he cherished. "On the bed, Shane."

"Like I'm gonna argue?" He climbed on the bed and stopped in the middle on all fours. His body trembled with what Brig hoped was need as strong as his own.

What else could it have been after that amazing blowjob he delivered earlier? "On your back. I wanna see your face when I push into you for the first time. When you feel my cock filling you. But, I need you to give me a little guidance here. I've never done this and I don't wanna hurt you."

"You ever fucked a woman in the ass?"

Shit was that curiosity? Or was he maybe a little jealous? "Yeah, I've tried it a few times. The ones that were into it seemed to like it."

"Then you got this." Shane grinned and waved him over. "Come on and ride me cowboy. I've been waiting a long damn time to feel you inside of me."

"Fuck yeah." He tossed the tube on the bed and crawled over Shane. He snagged his lips in another soul searing kiss and let everything else fade away. This was about love, pure and simple. Nothing else mattered.

They parted slightly, both breathing heavy. "I'm sorry I took so long to man up."

"I shouldn't have hid who I am from you. Maybe you would have told me sooner." Shane laid his hand along Brig's face, "But I'm not sorry I finally said something. No more regrets."

"No more. Your mine now." Brig grabbed the lube and squirted some on his fingers. Kneeling between his legs he slipped one digit past his tight pucker. He worked it in and out until he could add a second. Then he started stretching the orifice until Shane moaned with need.

"Please. Fuck me."

He grunted and kept working his fingers in and out. Then he added a third.

"God, Brig. Please." His hips flexed, tried to drive him deeper.

He let his hand swing down and slap the side of his ass. "I'm the one doing the fucking here. Lesson number one. I'm in charge in here. Can you handle that?"

A moment of indecision danced across Shane's face and then he grinned. "Yes, sir."

"Good. Now hush up so I can get my dick in your tight hole." Oh yeah. He knew back in college that Shane had submissive tendencies. Suited him just fine since he was a bit of a control freak. He pulled his fingers out and lubed up his cock. Then he took in the view of that stretched hole, open and ready to receive him and everything felt right for the first time ever. He was right where he was supposed to be.

On that note, he pressed the head of his cock against the hole and pressed in. Shane moaned as he shoved past the tight ring of muscle and sank into him one slow inch at a time. Face to face they stayed put and stared into each other's eyes. "Feels better than I ever imagined."

"Same goes, now please fuck me."

So he did. He pounded into his real life wet dream until the need to come buzzed up through his balls, along his spine, and out through his dick. The tightness gripped him tighter as he spewed and he glanced down to watch Shane shoot all over his stomach. So fucking hot.

Spent, he collapsed on top of his friend and now lover. "Best sex ever."

"Hell yeah. Though I was pretty sure you were gonna bust out some rope at one point."

"Who said I won't?" Brig grinned as he levered up leaving their bodies joined. "I'm pretty sure I've got a piggin' string somewhere."

The End

# Stealing His Cowgirl's Heart

*One Night With A Cowboy*
Book 5
**Sorcha Mowbray**

# Chapter One

MJ stared at the blank form on her computer screen. First question: *Physically describe your ideal man.* Well, damn. Unbidden, an image of a lean muscular boy with dark hair and even darker eyes popped into her head. She really wanted to ignore it, but since she hadn't done that in damn near ten years she knew better than to think she would do it now. Nope. Not likely to happen.

So she typed in the description. Tall, dark hair, dark eyes. She chewed her lip for a minute and then smiled to herself. Muscular, wide shoulders, physically fit. There, he never had wide shoulders. He was always on the lean side and had spent more time lifting an illegal can of beer than weights.

Next question. She looked at the words and stopped to think. *What kind of activities should he enjoy?* Well, she owned a ranch. Horseback riding, off-roading, hiking—her hands paused over the keyboard. Fuck it, she should be honest. Shooting guns, swimming, and cross-fit training.

She'd never been a shrinking violet, but after she found herself alone in the world with nobody to rely on but herself she realized she had to be able to do everything she asked of her ranch hands. That meant pleasantly plump Mary Jane had to go. In her place, MJ—woman rancher—was carved. Every muscle, every curve was earned by hard work both on the ranch and in the gym. Well, her equivalent of a gym. The barn. She discovered that by using things she had around the place she could design a workout that would make her stronger, faster, and all around a better rancher.

Next question. *Describe your ideal man's personality.* She snorted. He would be honest. No bullshit allowed. She'd had enough of that to last her a lifetime before she'd even turned eighteen. Oh, and he had to be loyal. She didn't need pretty words. She needed a man.

She went through and answered the questions about herself until she got to the end of the questionnaire. For a minute she looked back over all her answers and then she hit submit. A moment later a box popped up on her screen.

*Thank you for submitting your profile to Soul Mates Dating. We are seeking out your perfect match. Don't be discouraged, we will be in touch with you soon.*

She sighed. Figures they needed time. With a few clicks she shutdown her computer and pushed away from the glowing screen. It was after ten o'clock and she should have been in bed an hour ago. The animals wouldn't care for themselves and that meant she had to be up before sunrise. After chores she would squeeze her workout in and then the rest of the day was spent with her ranch hands fixing fence, haying the fields, and feeding the cattle. She wanted to hate her daddy for leaving her alone in the world with a ranch to run, but she knew she wouldn't be happy anywhere else. And how could she hate the one man who loved her without conditions? Besides, it was wrong to think ill of the dead.

The house lay quiet, too quiet, but there wasn't much she could do about it until that dating site got back to her. She climbed the stairs to her bedroom and went about getting ready for bed. Her phone dinged, indicating she had a new email. Certain it was the ladies league asking for more help with one of their ridiculous events—why they thought she had time or inclination to join them she couldn't figure out—she simply set the phone on vibrate for the night. She could tell them no in the morning.

Friday dragged on, slow as molasses. Not that she'd ever eaten any, but it seemed fitting for the slow crawl of her day. By lunch time she was ready to call it quits, but honestly what was the point? If she threw in the towel she'd end up sitting in her house starring at the TV or aimlessly surfing the web. She damn sure wouldn't be doing the bookkeeping, no matter how badly it needed to be done. So, she sat down to eat a sandwich and pulled her phone out of her pocket. She looked at her email and saw she had two messages. As expected, the ladies league had sent her another invitation. She snorted. Then she realized that message had come in mid-morning. So, she looked again and saw the message from the night before had been from the dating service. She clicked on the icon, expecting another email telling her they were looking for her match, but instead the message said something completely different.

*Dear MJ,*

*We are pleased to tell you we have found your perfect match. Saturday night you and your date will meet at The Bucking Bronco for dinner, drinks, and dancing. He will be wearing a blue shirt with a brown Resistol. Please be there at 7pm and wearing red. I hope you enjoy your evening.*

*Sincerely,*

*Selena Markham*

*President and CEO*

*Soul Mates Dating*

Her heart skipped a few beats. That had been fast. She forgot her sandwich and headed into her bedroom to see if she even owned anything red. You would think with blonde hair and blue eyes, she would own one article of clothing that was red. But being a practical girl, she mostly stuck to dark colors. They hid both dirt and wear well. She bit her lip and made the most impulsive decision of her life since the time she asked Nathanial Keller to the Sadie Hawkins dance her junior year.

Had she known then the hell he'd put her through, she would have skipped it all together. Never would have asked him. Never would have gone. Then, maybe, she would have actually met someone who could steal her heart. Then, maybe, she wouldn't be alone.

Keys in hand, she called out to Frank, her foreman. "Headed in to town to run some errands. Need anything?"

He was by all accounts a handsome man. At least, he seemed to attract a lot of female attention. The single ladies of Shady Gulch seemed unabashed about asking her if he was single on a regular basis. Of course, since he worked for her, she didn't know much about his personal life. She didn't ask. And he had long ago stopped asking about hers. "Can you grab five sacks of feed? We're running low and the monthly order won't be in until next week."

"You got it. I won't be back before sunset, so see you tomorrow." She plopped her straw Stetson on her head and slid behind the wheel of her truck. She needed something nice-looking to wear and maybe even some fancy underthings. She had always been a simple cotton girl, but she figured if she was turning over a new leaf she needed to flip the whole damn thing over, not just lift up the edge.

So, an hour later, thanks to the old man Harper's combine, she was in downtown Shady Gulch and standing in Eloise's Ladies Wear. It wasn't much, but Eloise at least had some things that had ruffles and even some lace. Resisting the urge to head straight to the sale rack, MJ tried sifting through some dresses in her size.

"Well, hello Mary Jane." Eloise Parker was the same as she'd always been. Seemingly sweet, but with an undercurrent of superiority that left one with a bitter taste in their mouth. Kind of like a pink packet of sweetener.

"Eloise." She kept sliding hangers from left to right on the rack in hopes she'd come across something she could try on just to get away from the woman.

"Why, what brings you in to the shop?" She smiled and blinked.

"I need a red dress," MJ mumbled as she continued moving hangers. Something red caught her eye and she snatched it up. "This will do."

Shit this had turned out to be harder than she thought. She hadn't accounted for the town busybody when she decided to come to town and go shopping.

"Got a hot date?" The harpy had the nerve to smirk as though the idea that she had a date, hot or otherwise, was unbelievable.

Of course, she knew what the girls had said about her behind her back after Nathanial bolted from town. She was frigid. She couldn't keep a man.

Something was wrong with her. There were all kinds of variations to the story, but in the end they all held her responsible for running off Nathanial. And to be honest, she was worried it might have been true. At least for a while. Eventually she figured out whatever had happened, it wasn't about her. So, she stiffened her spine and looked the bitch in her dull brown eyes. "As a matter of fact, I do."

The look of utter shock on Eloise's face sent a wave of satisfaction through MJ.

After a moment of sputtering like a landed fish, the tall blonde recovered. "Well then, you need to be looking over here. Not at those stuffy dresses I stock for my mother and her friends."

After getting past her own round of surprise, MJ followed her guide over to another rack where the dresses seemed to come with far less material included. "Oh, Eloise. I dunno."

The stylishly dressed woman looked her up and down. "I do. If you've got a date you don't want to look like you've played dress up in your grandma's leftover dresses." Her gaze drifted down over dusty jeans and worn in boots. "I assume you don't plan on going straight from the field to meet him?"

"Of course not." MJ wanted to turn on her heel and stomp out, but however rude she was, the woman had a point. She'd come to buy a dress so she would look more feminine. So she would feel like a woman. "Show me something in red."

Eloise smiled and nodded. Five minutes later, MJ found herself shoved into a dressing room with a pile of red dresses. For half an hour she tried on one after another. Each one was either shot down by her or by Eloise. A few she flat out refused to leave the dressing room in. They had barely qualified as dresses considering her backside almost hung out of them. Finally, with the last dress they both agreed she'd found a winner. Cut with a fuller skirt, but in a light cotton material with a red floral print it was the perfect summer sundress and it hit just above her knees. She had the shiny black cowboy boots her daddy had bought her in hopes she'd go out dancing, but then he'd died and going dancing seemed unimportant. After she bought the dress, she headed across the street to the new lingerie shop that had opened last year.

She'd never been in it, for obvious reasons. She usually got what she needed at the feed store. Jeans, work shirts, boots, and sensible cotton underwear that didn't chafe and lasted forever.

She walked in the shop and stopped dead in her tracks when confronted by the riot of frills and color. This was just not *her*. She spun around and took one step toward the door she'd just come in when a voice called out. "Hello! Can I help you with something?"

MJ whipped back around and clutched her new dress to her chest. "Um. No. Sorry. I was, uh…just leaving."

The woman smiled a genuinely sweet smile, glanced down at the dress in her hands, the state of the clothes she wore and then at the panic she knew was plain on her face. "You need something feminine to go with that new dress I bet."

She shook her head, the need to get out of the frilly shop and in to the feed store where she was on solid ground damn near brought her to her knees. "No. Really. I—"

"Please. I know all the colors and lace is overwhelming compared to the feed store where everything comes in white cotton. But I promise, if you let me help you, you won't regret it."

Her smile was so sweet and welcoming, MJ finally gave in. "Ok. Sorry, I panicked."

"You aren't the first rancher that's wandered in here and nearly fainted from feminine overload. And the men are worse." She laughed lightly and held out her hand. "I'm Caroline."

MJ relaxed a bit. "MJ. I own the Bar F, halfway between here and Austin."

"Well, MJ. It's nice to meet you. Let's find you a bra and panties to go with your dress." She placed a hand on the garment bag expectantly. "May I?"

"Sure." MJ handed over her dress and before she knew it she'd left with both new underthings…red lacy underthings, and a promise to have lunch with Caroline the next week.

By the time she'd gotten the five bags of feed loaded it was sunset and she was hungry. So she headed over to The Bucking Bronco for dinner. Other than Linda's Diner it was the only other place to eat in town, and she needed a beer. Besides, it was too early for the bar side to be busy, so she shouldn't run in to anyone she knew.

Even if she did, it wasn't like they hadn't seen her in her dirt crusted work clothes before. Right?

# Chapter Two

Nate sat at the bar in The Bucking Bronco and looked at the email on his phone once more. He'd been home all of a week and out of his cast for two. He was there to get some rest and relaxation while he got his physical conditioning started again so he could get back to work. Three months off had him going stir crazy and he still had another month before they'd even let him start training with his Seal Team again. And who knew how long after that before they let him go on a mission.

At least he hadn't gone to pot over the last few months. A daily rigorous routine of sit-ups, dips, and anything else he could manage without using his right leg had fought off his propensity to run to fat. Of course, sitting in a bar drinking a beer and eating pretzels wasn't really helping. He could get away with it every so often when he was active, but from the sidelines it was dangerous.

But apparently danger must be his drug of choice since he hadn't balked at the idea of a blind date courtesy of Soul Mates Dating and his best friend Andy "Hot Rod" Rodderson. What the hell the man had been thinking was beyond him. No wait, he knew what he was thinking. He was deliriously in love, so everyone should be. Nate shook his head.

He'd trod that path once long ago and it led him straight to Idiotsville and a judge. Love made a man stupid. Hence, Hot Rod's gift.

The door to the bar/restaurant opened and slapped shut. Since it was too early for anyone interesting to be coming in the place, he didn't bother to turn around. Not even when a lightly feminine fragrance of lilies and fresh air with a tang of manure wafted under his nose. He grinned to himself. Only in Shady Gulch could an undertone of shit be considered part of a feminine scent. Back in Virginia the women came slick and slicker. And all hell would have broken loose if one of them thought their expensive perfume held a note of horse dung.

He took a swig from his beer and set it down on the bar.

"Can I get a menu for the restaurant on this side?" A smoky female voice asked the bartender.

"Sure thing, MJ." The bartender walked over to the register, grabbed a menu and handed it to the woman who sat a few seats to his left. He turned to get a better look as the blonde set her straw cowboy hat on the bar, and his heart nearly leapt out of his chest. MJ? As in Mary Jane Martin? He couldn't help but stare. Sure, he figured he'd run in to her at some point while he was there, but he hadn't expected to see her so soon. Or in The Bucking Bronco.

He was about to stand up and slide down when a group of ranch hands rolled in to the bar and sucked up the space between them. In that moment he decided fate was giving him a reprieve from facing his own personal demons. So he stayed where he was hidden behind a group of cowboys. One of the guys dropped some money in the juke box and played the classic George Straight song, *All My Exes Live in Texas.*

He finished off his beer and decided it was time to go. As he stood he noticed two of the cowboys crowding MJ. To say the least, she looked uncomfortable. His gut twisted up because he knew he couldn't let it go. Despite ten years away from Shady Gulch and all the women who had graced his bed over the years, this one still held a special place in his heart. First love.

Her voice rose above the music as she stood up to deal with the two men harassing her. "I said I don't want to dance, Calvin."

"Come on, MJ. You're the only woman in the place. We just want to take you for a spin." The cowboy, who Nate supposed women would call handsome, grinned and tried to flirt.

"I know your mama taught you better than that. When a woman says no, she means no, and you should respect that whether it's dancing or...or..." her cheeks flushed bright red and her gaze dropped to the floor as her hands fisted at her sides.

"Or something else?" The other one, a dark haired man, finished for her.

MJ glared at the cowboy, who smirked like a naughty boy trying to brazen his way out of trouble. Without looking away from the two troublesome men, MJ called out to the bartender. "Make that order to go."

"Sure thing MJ." The woman shuffled off, almost relieved to be leaving the room.

The one she'd called Calvin stepped in closer, pinning her against the bar. "You can't really be as cold as they say, MJ. Why don't me, you, and Bart here, go have us a little rodeo. Then we can deny what people are saying for you."

That was it. Nate had heard more than enough. "Sorry boys, but the lady said no already." He stepped up to her open side and with a firm grip tugged her to his side and away from the two bullies.

"Nathanial?" Shock widened her eyes making the big blue iris' look even bluer than he remembered.

"Hey, babe." He leaned down, pressed a kiss to her cheek and whispered in her ear. "Just go along with me."

"Who the hell are you?" The dark haired one eyed him suspiciously.

"Her boyfriend." Ten years ago, maybe.

They both laughed. MJ stared at the floor so hard he thought she might be trying to figure out a way to drill through it and escape.

"MJ ain't ever had a boyfriend," Calvin said. He crossed his arms and glared as though he were the authority.

The bartender reappeared and plopped the bag of food to go on the bar. "Here you go, MJ."

She reached over grabbed the food and mumbled a thanks before she walked away.

Nate glared at the young men, certainly younger than him, and then followed MJ out of the bar. "Excuse us."

The rest of the cowboys watched as they departed the bar. Out in the parking lot MJ was halfway to her truck by the time he caught up with her. "Hey there, Mary Jane."

She continued to beeline to the same old truck she'd driven in high school.

"Wait a minute." He called out hoping she just hadn't heard him. But no, the stubborn woman still wouldn't stop. Then she was in the cab and the door locked before he could stop her. He knocked on the window as she cranked the engine. But nothing happened. The thing sputtered and coughed and then died. She tried again. And again the engine wouldn't cooperate. Still separated by a pane of glass he watched the silent movie unfold. She gripped the wheel tight, her knuckles blanching white, and then dropped her forehead against the hard plastic circle. The sexy woman sat there ignoring him as if she hoped he would leave, but there was no way he would do that when she was clearly stranded.

He knocked on the window and tried again. "MJ, open the door."

"Can't you please go away?" Her voice came out muffled, but strong enough to be heard through the glass.

"Babe, let me help you." He wanted to do more than help her. Despite having to chase her across the lot, he'd had time to notice just how good she looked in her muck covered jeans. Not painted on like some cowgirl floozy, but she filled them out real nice. Nicer than he remembered from high school. "I have my truck here. I can give you a jump."

She looked up, defeat in her gaze. Despite the road noise, he heard the distinctive click of her hood release and then she opened her door. "Go get your truck. I've got cables."

Nate hesitated, he'd long ago gotten accustomed to giving orders on his squad, and in particular he remembered Mary Jane being shy. It was why he'd been so shocked when she asked him to the Sadie Hawkins dance. But apparently in the intervening years, she'd discovered a bit more of that spine he knew she'd had. He liked to think he'd helped her find some of that while they were dating. "Hang tight."

"It's not like I'm going anywhere." Her sassy little comeback made him smile as he jogged off toward his ride.

A few minutes later he had her jumped and ready to go. She slammed the hood closed, tossed her cables in the cab under the seat and made to climb in the truck. He reached out and set a hand on her arm only to feel the same jolt of awareness he remembered every time he fantasized about stripping her naked. Pushing the cock hardening thought aside, he said, "Hang on. I'm gonna follow you home to be sure you get there safe."

"No." She pressed her lips together into a flat, stubborn line.

"You can't stop me, MJ."

The sun dipped below the horizon and a couple trucks pulled into the parking lot now that the work day was over officially. She glanced around as though she was worried about who would see her talking to him in the parking lot of the local bar.

He tried again. "Please. I'd like to talk to you for a minute, but I'd rather not do it here."

Her chin tipped up and her eyes flashed in the dying light. "What's wrong, Nathanial? Embarrassed to be seen with me?"

Awe, hell. She really had become an ornery woman. "Hell, no. But I do prefer this to be a private conversation instead of one between you, me, and half of Shady Gulch."

She seemed to consider his words for a minute. "You're not gonna let this go, are you?"

Something angry flashed in her eyes and then disappeared. In its place settled resignation and wariness. But she was right. He wasn't going to let this go. "No. There are some things I need to say to you. And some explanations I owe you."

She heaved a sigh and then sat in her truck. "Fine. Follow me to the ranch. My foreman lives on site, but he should keep to himself unless I holler."

Nate nodded. "Got it, privacy, but help is there if you need it."

"Been a long time, Nathanial. And you just up and walked out of my life at the drop of a dime. Trust is not something I have a surplus of at the moment." She slanted one corner of her mouth up.

"I get it. No worries, MJ." He nodded and turned to his truck. "Even if you lose me, I know where your place is still. I'll find you." And with a sense of determination he hadn't realized he had, he climbed in his truck and followed her out to her spread.

# Chapter Three

**M**J pulled into her drive and tried to get ahold of her rioting emotions. On one hand she wanted to kill Nathanial for just showing back up in her life like he hadn't walked out ten years earlier. On the other hand, parts of her body she thought long closed for business had fired back online when he touched her. Add to her swirl of emotions the fact she had her first date in ten years scheduled for the next night, and she was downright angry. Screw him for strolling back into her life and screwing things up.

But then she realized how silly her reaction was. The man hadn't said a word about having come back for her. In fact all he said was he owed her some explanations. She needed to rein in the crazy in her head, hear the man out, and get on with her life. No matter how damn sexy he'd looked looming over her while he fended off Calvin and Greg.

She stopped in front of her house, shut the truck off, and grabbed her food while leaving her earlier purchases in the cab. Nathanial pulled up right behind her in a black pickup truck. Staunchly ignoring her increased heart rate, she flipped her tailgate down, sat, and pulled out her food.

He stepped over to her and stopped. "Mind if I sit?"

She glanced at her tailgate and considered saying no. In the end, good manners won out. "Nope." He settled down next to her and she held her to-go plate toward him. "Fry?"

"No thanks. I'm good." He crossed his arms and leaned against the side of the truck. "MJ, huh? That's different."

She wanted to snort, but managed to contain herself. "A lot changed after you left. That happens over a decade."

"I know. I go by Nate now." His voice held a tinge of sadness.

"Huh. It fits you now. You're"—she waved a fry in his direction—"so much bigger now. A shorter name fits."

He laughed. "Did you just call me a meathead?"

She blushed, though he wouldn't be able to see it in the moonlight. "No. Nathanial just…" She looked off into the darkness. "Nathanial was the boy I knew, not the man that stands here."

"I get that. That boy changed a lot along the way. Maybe it had started back when you and I dated? I don't know. But it definitely happened when I hit boot camp."

Silence descended. Uncomfortable, MJ shoved a fry into her mouth and chewed. There was a time when she would have chattered on when he got quiet. Now, she didn't know what to say. Finally, she had to know. "What happened?"

"A lot. Most of it stupid, some of it not. You and I were hot and heavy. Things had gone south at home with my mom. You knew she drank heavy, hell all of Shady Gulch knew that. But, then she got mixed up with some asshole who introduced her to coke. She hid it pretty well until he bailed, leaving her with a habit she couldn't afford. She started stealing." He sighed.

In the moonlight, she could see his profile as he stared at the ground. "When the cops came to the house looking for the jewelry she took from one of the houses she cleaned, I refused to let her go down for theft. I took the arrest. She came and got me, crying about how sorry she was and how she'd make it right, but by the time it went to court it was too late. The judge guessed at what had happened, took one look at my mom in the court room and called me into chambers with the attorneys. He offered me a deal. No record, but I had to enlist. Didn't matter which service, he said as long as I got out of town. So I took it. They took me from the courthouse straight to the recruiter's office where I signed on and shipped out immediately. No time to say anything to anyone."

MJ let his words sink in past all the hurt. It wasn't her. She hadn't done anything to cause him to leave. "Wow, that must have been hard."

He looked up from the ground. "Leaving you was the hardest part."

Silence settled again. MJ debated saying something about that last statement, and Nate—well, who knew what might be rolling around in his head. In the end, her need to know won out over any sense of invasion of privacy. "You never called, wrote, anything. Why?"

"I was embarrassed about my mom, and in the end I thought I could protect you from being tainted with my family drama. I didn't want Shady Gulch talking about your boyfriend's junkie mom. I thought if I disappeared there wouldn't be anything to talk about."

"Well, it sort of worked. Guess the judge and lawyers had the records sealed or erased or whatever. Because nobody ever knew anything except you joined the Navy and left without a word. Then your mom disappeared for a few months. When she came back she was clean and sober."

"Yeah, it made what I did worth it." She couldn't help but flinch at his statement. But, then he looked up and their gazes locked. "Or almost worth it. Walking away from you is my biggest regret." He lifted a hand as though he wanted to touch her.

"Well." She jumped up from the back of the truck and spun around to gather her forgotten food. "It's getting late."

Despite the darkness, she swore she caught a flash of hurt in his eyes at her sudden movement.

"Yeah, I guess so." He stood up and turned to her.

Every instinct told her no hugs. No touching. But he closed the distance anyway despite the take out container she held awkwardly between them. And, as she suspected, the contact lit up her senses like it was the Fourth of July. She closed her eyes and drew in a deep breath as she tried to absorb what his touch felt like one last time. Later, much later she'd box the memory up and tuck it away.

"Thanks for listening." His whispered words caressed the shell of her ear and only added to the internal fireworks.

"You're welcome." And then he pulled away.

Nate crossed the space between their trucks and opened the door to his black rig. The need to say something, to forgive him spiked through her

126

chest like an early morning ray of sunshine. "Nate?"

He stopped and looked back at her.

"For what it's worth, I think you did the right thing for your mom."

"Thanks, MJ."

And then he climbed in the cab, turned the engine over and retreated the same way he had arrived.

Emotionally lost after such an intense conversation, she reached in her truck, pulled out her dress and fancy new undies, and trudged through the front door. The past felt like another occupant of her house at the moment. A living breathing thing that wanted her attention. Needed her attention. Suddenly not sure what she felt for Nate, feeling like the past no longer remained where she'd left it, and questioning the wisdom of going on a blind date the next night; she carefully put everything away. How could she even give the guy a fair shake when all she could think about was Nate and everything he'd done. For his mom. For her.

Sure, he was misguided in the notion that he could protect her by leaving. But, he clearly hadn't meant to hurt her. And he hadn't had a choice about going. In the end it wasn't his fault she struggled to let go. That she compared every man she met to Nathanial.

And, wow. Nate was not Nathanial. The boy had become a man, a very real, very sexy man. She sighed, but he didn't belong to her anymore. And she wasn't sure she could hold the man the way she had the boy.

Yep, it was best she tried to move on. Stick with the plan. Go on her date.

# Chapter Four

N ate found himself sitting in the Bucking Bronco for the second time in two days. Alone. But, he hoped, not for long. Canceling his date had been a close thing after running into MJ. That woman remained firmly lodged in his heart. Not that he'd tried too hard to root her out. Nope. He liked her just fine there. Problem was, it seemed to be the only place she actually worked in his life.

Especially now.

With the Bar F under her control her ties to home were even stronger than back when they'd been young and in love. More so than when he'd walked out on her. She was settled in a way that broke his heart, because once he had imagined being settled by her side. An unstoppable duo taking on the world, or maybe just their little patch of it. Instead they were ripped apart, and in an attempt to protect her he let the wound scar over.

Seeing her hadn't changed a thing because he had no choice but to leave again. Which meant, despite how badly he'd wanted to take her in his arms and kiss her until she forgot how to breathe, she was right to keep her distance. Right to try and move on with her life. Hell, for all he knew, she already had one. His chest constricted and the urge to punch something rode him hard. The idea of another man with his hands on MJ had him seeing red. No matter what that punk Calvin had said, she never confirmed or denied the truth of his statement. He took a deep breath and let the misplaced fury go. After all, he had no right.

He hadn't been a monk in the ten years since MJ, but no one had even come close to lighting his fire like she did. Or had. And here he was, out on a blind date. Damn he was such a hypocrite. And a total fool. His gut tightened, the beer turned to sawdust in his mouth, and a sudden need to escape overwhelmed him. This was a bad idea. He'd have to wait until he was back in Virginia to try dating.

He stood to leave when a flash of red caught his eye at the door. Then the crowd shifted and he realized it was the shirt of some cowboy all slicked up for a night on the town. Relief swept through him as he realized he still had time to escape. He took a step toward the exit when a woman in a red dress and shiny black cowboy boots stepped inside the door.

*Shit.*

As though he had no self-control, wasn't a fucking Navy Seal, his gaze swept upward from her slim legs, to her softly flared hips, past firm round breasts, to find sky blue eyes opened wide in surprise. A perfect O formed on her lips—sexy red tinted lips with a sheen of gloss. And then in a whirl of blond hair, MJ spun around and bolted back the way she'd come.

*Fuck.*

"MJ, wait!" He raced after her, bound and determined to catch her once again. Only difference was, this time he knew when he caught her, he'd never let her go. Fate had spoken loud and clear. Maybe it was time they both listened to her instead of everyone else.

He stormed outside to the quickly filling parking lot and caught a glimpse of red as it slipped around the bed of a truck. He darted off in that direction hoping like hell it was the woman he was after. Within a few strides, he had her in his sights, so ignoring the pain searing though his thigh as he pushed his weakened leg to the limits, he broke out into a run. He caught her halfway across the parking lot this time. With a firm grip on her arm, he got her to slow down and then stop. "Babe, hold on a minute."

"No. No babe. No holding on. I c-can't do this, Nate." Her chest heaved with either exertion or emotion. For a moment he wasn't sure which and then the first tear trickled down her cheek. His heart squeezed in his chest.

"MJ, please. I didn't know you were my date." His gaze searched her face, desperate for her to believe him.

"Soul Mates didn't tell you my name either?"

"No, they just said you'd be wearing a red dress and that I was to wear a blue shirt and brown Resistol." He grinned. "Had to go buy the damn hat. All I wear now are baseball caps and uniform gear."

A smile flitted across her oh so tempting lips. But then it was gone. "It doesn't change the outcome of all this. I can't do this. I've worked too hard to get over you. I finally gave up on you riding in to rescue me like some white knight. This was to be my first big step toward my future and here you are, a wrench in my works. Damn you, it's not fair." And she spun around as her shoulders shuddered.

He wrapped his arms around her from behind, desperately needing to comfort her somehow. "Please, babe. Don't cry. I can't explain this, except to recognize that fate seems to be throwing us together." He gently turned her back around to face him. She pressed her tear soaked face against his chest and wrapped her arms around his body, and it felt damn good. He took a moment to revel in the feel of her in his arms and then he leaned back so he could see her blue eyes in the moonlight.

"Don't look. My makeup must be ruined and I can feel how swollen my eyes are." She clung to him tighter.

He tipped her chin up with a finger and made her look at him. "You've always been beautiful to me. That hasn't changed in the last ten years. Probably won't change in the next fifty."

She rolled her eyes. "You always were godawful corny."

"Like you said somethings never change." *Like my love for you.* It felt good to acknowledge how he felt, even if only to himself. He fully intended to tell her later, but for now he just needed to get her to calm down and give them a chance.

"Oh, Nate. Even a week ago I would have leapt into your arms. Forgiven you anything, if you simply showed up and said you wanted me. But now? This week? I can't do it. I can't just let you waltz back into my life only to turn around and leave again."

"I'm here for a while and then, when I go back I want to take you with me. No rescue, but maybe give us a chance to rediscover what we had?"

"Nate, are you even listening to me? I won't do this. I'm sorry." She pulled

130

out of his embrace and hustled toward her truck.

He stood rooted to the ground and watched as the woman he loved walked away from him, from them. In his head he knew she only tried to protect herself, but his heart roared against the loss. However temporary it would be. If their aborted date told him anything, it was that they belonged together and he would do whatever it took to make sure that happened. The question was, how hard would MJ fight him? Didn't matter. If he had to, he'd steal his cowgirl's heart.

# Chapter Five

**M**J slammed the stupid wrench on the ground next to the broken tractor. She'd learned the hard way that despite its weight a wrench could bounce off another hard surface and hit you in the face. It was one thing to be stupid. It was a whole other thing to be reminded about your stupidity every time you looked in the mirror or ran in to a neighbor in town. And she was just tired enough from tossing and turning all night to do something really stupid. So, she slammed the hood back in place on the old tractor and walked away from the stubborn hunk of metal.

Sometimes walking away was the only smart choice.

Well, that was what she told herself last night as she laid—*alone*—in bed. She had wanted to throw her arms around Nate's neck and say yes to just about any damn thing the sexy man proposed, but in the end her sense of self-preservation won out. There was no way she could survive another parting from him. And as much as sex sounded good, she also knew that she couldn't sleep with him without her heart coming along for the ride.

Sometimes walking away was the only smart choice.

She headed up to the house to fix some lunch. Maybe after she ate she could solve the mystery of the tractor. She damn sure couldn't solve her other issue.

As she neared the main house she saw two men standing by the porch talking. She instantly recognized both men, but couldn't figure out why one of them was there. Her empty stomach did a slow roll as Nate's chiseled features came into focus. His strong jaw stubbled with dark hair that matched his head, wide muscular shoulders that looked like they could carry the weight of the world on them, and thick forearms that hinted at strong hands and an iron grip.

She'd read enough erotica to have a few ideas about what he might do with that strong grip if she ever let him. With a groan she shoved the forbidden thoughts back where they belonged. She had no business fantasizing about his fist in her hair as he rode her hard from behind. None whatsoever.

Frank turned around as Nate straightened up from his lean against the bannister. She sure hoped they'd assume the heat in her cheeks was from the sun and not her thoughts. Her deliciously naughty thoughts.

"MJ, Nate here says you know each other." Frank crossed his arms over his chest. Funny, she could see his shoulders and arms were as well built as Nate's, but for whatever reason they did nothing to make her heart skip a beat or her thoughts grow decidedly wicked.

"I know him. Just not sure why he's here." She stopped next to the man she'd worked side by side with for nine years.

"I'm here to take you to lunch." Nate smiled at her, and damn her soul if she didn't want to melt right there.

She snorted, as much to annoy him as to buy herself a moment. "I don't remember agreeing to have lunch with you."

"Didn't ask." He winked at her.

The man had some audacity. She wanted to be mad, but a part of her squealed and did a happy dance. Stupid girl.

"Maybe you should have." She looked pointedly down at her grease smeared coveralls and muck covered boots.

"No way, babe. Then you would have made some excuse why you couldn't eat with me." Nate's gaze said, I dare you to disagree.

Frank, poor man, stood there alternating his confused stare between her and Nate. He looked so flummoxed by the light, but slightly edgy banter, that she took pity on the man. "Frank, could you give us a minute?"

"You sure, MJ? If you don't want this guy here I am happy to toss him off the property." He gave Nate a stare that said he meant business.

"Well, you could try to throw me off the property. But I should give you

133

fair warning. I win King of the Hill every time I play it with my Seal team."

Frank had started to smirk, but then his eyebrows shot up as he realized that whatever version of the childhood game his team played probably didn't meet friendly competition by normal standards.

"Thank you, Frank. He won't hurt me." *Well, at least not physically.* Her foreman and friend walked away, but turned back a few times to look. Once he was out of earshot, she turned to Nate and glared. "Was that really necessary?"

Nate played innocent. "What? He threatened me. I just warned him that I wasn't his average cowboy. Seemed only fair."

She sighed. Men were so ridiculous.

"Now, about lunch—"

"No lunch. I'm not dressed to go anywhere public not to mention I specifically told you last night I wouldn't do this." She crossed her arms over her chest. Of course she realized after it was too late, that all that did was squish her boobs together and lift her cleavage for him.

"As I tried to say, I brought a picnic feast for two and a blanket. So, we can do it here in the front yard, or I hoped we could take your dad's old four wheelers out to that field by the stream." He waited for her to say something.

"No." Why did he have to make this so hard?

"Well, that wasn't a yes or no question. But I do appreciate your consistency." He winked at her, again. "Now, if I remember things right, you keep them in the barn." He leaned over, grabbed the previously hidden basket from the porch and a blanket. With both things in his hand, he started across the yard.

"Damn it, Nate." She chased after him.

He swung the barn door open with one hand and walked into the dim interior. She stopped inside the door and waited to see what he would do. It was like time had stopped and it was the summer before he left. He set everything on the back of one of the two seater vehicles and then tossed her a sexy grin as he waived her over.

She shook her head. No way.

"MJ, don't make me carry you over here." His grin spread and she swore he maybe hoped she would.

"Even if I come over there, it doesn't mean I'm getting on that thing with you."

"Damn it woman. It's lunch. You've gotta eat don't you?"

Shit. When did he start making sense? But if she went with him, there had to be ground rules. If she didn't have rules she would get in even more trouble than she already was. "Fine, I'll eat. But there will be rules."

The man grinned the most beatific, shit eating grin she'd ever seen. "I can do rules."

"No touching." She couldn't take the sensory torture.

"No. You have to touch me when we ride out to the spot. It's not safe and I won't compromise on your safety." His firm declaration on behalf of her well being sent a little thrill through her.

"Fine. I can touch you." She kicked a clod of dirt with the toe of her boot. "No talking."

"Woman, that's ridiculous and you know it."

It was, but seriously he could have read her the ag report and she would get turned on. "All right. No dirty talk."

For a moment he looked mutinous, but then he relented. "Agreed. No dirty talk. That means no talk of pussies or cocks. Of mine sliding into yours. No mention of me sucking on the ripe tips of your breasts. No discussing me licking and sucking on your—"

"Nate!" Holy hell was that a mini heat wave that just rolled through the cool dimness of the barn?

"Got it." He offered her a wicked, wicked grin.

"And absolutely no getting naked." There. He couldn't talk her around that one.

And he couldn't. He even looked disappointed she'd thought of it. "Fine no getting naked."

Satisfied she'd made her point, she crossed the barn and climbed on the back of the four wheeler. "Okay. Let's go."

He threw a leg over the saddle of the vehicle and cranked the engine to life. It wouldn't take them long to reach the pasture he mentioned. So she wrapped her arms around his strong midsection and settled in to enjoy the late fall warmth as they zipped across her land. Now she just had to figure out how to survive lunch with the man she loved.

# Chapter Six

Nate was both elated and kind of worried about his impromptu lunch. It had seemed like a great idea that morning. After MJ declared all her rules, he wasn't sure how he could make his plan work the way he originally envisioned. He'd laid in bed and pictured them snuggled on a blanket in the fall sunshine while he fed her bits of food and teased her with kisses. If things were going really well they'd get naked and swim and well then…things might happen. He felt certain if he could remind her how good they were together in bed and out, the rest would work itself out.

Now she had set up all kinds of limitations. Ornery woman.

For the moment, he relished the feel of her arms wrapped around him as they tore across her lands. It was beautiful scenery. Not as breathtaking as the woman behind him, but still inspiring.

The tree by the creek came into view and he angled toward their old spot. They had spent more than one summer night out there alone, necking, and then later making love. Sex in the outdoors had definitely been one thing he missed. Where he lived was far too built up for those kinds of outdoor activities.

They came to a stop, and she practically leapt off the machine. He stifled the sense of disappointment and focused on spending time with her. She might not give him another opportunity to show her how they could be.

"Why don't you spread out the blanket and I'll bring over the basket." He tossed her the old quilt he'd dug out of his mom's linen closet. He hadn't told her he was taking it, and hoped it wasn't some kind of keepsake.

MJ spread the thing out but he drew up short as he realized it was his old Star Wars comforter from when he was a boy. Heat filled his cheeks. Very sexy. He wanted to curse.

"Need a hand there, Han?"

Her smirk warmed his heart. Teasing was good. "Han? Why not Luke? I'd make a great Jedi."

"Luke and Leia were related." And just like that her mouth clamped shut and she spun around, sat down, and pulled off her filthy boots.

He couldn't contain the grin that bit of information caused. But, he decided to let her off the hook. He set the basket down and opened the lid. "I wasn't sure what you liked, so I stopped by Linda's Diner and got a little of everything."

MJ turned back around and stared as he pulled out one container after another. "I thought you brought lunch for me, not the entire Bar F staff."

He shrugged. "Like I said. I wasn't sure what you liked. So you have your choice of sandwich: turkey, ham, or roast beef. Chicken or tuna salad. And a side salad. Oh and I brought plain, barbeque, and salt and vinegar chips too."

Everything sat arrayed on the blanket and she shook her head. "You're crazy."

"I think that goes without saying." Of course, his particular brand of crazy was a direct result of loving her. "Thirsty?"

Her eyes bulged as she stared at the basket. "Tell me you don't have a soda machine in there."

He laughed. Threw his head back and laughed until his sides hurt, and it felt so good. When he could finally speak he shook his head. "Nope, no soda machine. There's only one option if I remember right." And then he reached in and pulled out her favorite soda. Diet Dr. Pepper.

She stared at the can in his hand, then looked up at his face, and then back at the can. When the first tear fell, he set the can aside and reached for her. But, remembering her rules he pulled up short. "Babe, I really want to hold you right now, but you said no touching."

She wiped her eyes and sniffed. "I'm sorry, I'm fine. I swear. It's just that, well—you remembered my favorite soda."

"Are you kidding? I remember your favorite soda. Your favorite color. Blue, by the way. That this was your favorite spot to picnic. And that you without a doubt hate mornings." He let his gaze snare hers and refused to let go. "I remember what it's like to hold you. To love you. What it's like to make you smile, and how satisfying it is to make you laugh. I remember all the important things." Shit. Had he said too much? He hadn't wanted to come on so strong, but her surprise that he remembered something like her favorite soda kind of hurt even after he explained he hadn't wanted to go.

"Oh." Her cheeks grew red as she dropped her gaze to the infinity of space spread out beneath them.

He needed to switch gears again. "Now, what did you want to eat? I think it was always a toss-up between chicken salad and roast beef."

She smiled and looked up at him. "Roast beef. I had chicken salad yesterday."

They sat and ate in companionable silence as the sun rose overhead. Even though it was late October, the summer heat had not abated. After they ate he stretched out on the quilt and soaked up the sun that had peeked around the canopy of the tree. A glance over at MJ revealed she seemed as lethargic as he felt. When a trickle of sweat slid down his back between his shoulder blades, an idea occurred to him. She'd said no getting naked. She did not say he couldn't strip down to his underwear and take a swim in the creek. Mind you, it would be damn cold at this point in October. But it would be totally worth it to get wet and then lay in the sun to drip dry.

With a devilish sense of glee, he stood up and pulled off his hat. Then he jerked his shirt up over his head. At that point she snapped up to sitting.

"Nate, you agreed no getting naked." Her voice came out low and wary.

"Not getting naked. But I plan to cool off in the creek." He pulled off one boot, followed by the other. Then he pulled off his socks.

She started to relax and then he unbuckled his belt.

"Hey!"

"MJ, you can't expect me to swim in my jeans and then wear them home. Don't be heartless, babe." He gave her the puppy dog eyes he used to pull out when she got obstinate about something.

"I won't look." She turned the other way.

"Suit yourself." He called out and ran into the water no sooner than his pants hit the ground. "Woo! Hoo!"

The water was ice-fucking-cold. Like so cold he was pretty sure his nuts had relocated inside his body.

"You are certifiable." Her voice drew his attention, and he caught her looking.

He couldn't hide his smile. "We've covered that. Sure you don't want to join me? It's very refreshing."

"You mean it's cold as hell and you want to torture me." She remained firmly in place on their blanket.

"Ok. I'm about done anyway." And he thanked every one of the domestic gods that he had worn his only pair of white boxer briefs that morning.

As water sluiced down his body, he knew the damn things were all but transparent. It was why he never bought them anymore. After having stripped down to his skivvies in the field with his team, he learned black drawers equaled modesty even when wet.

When he hit the creek bank MJs eyes bulged out of her head, but she did not look away. Victory!

"Nate," she squealed.

"What, MJ?" He had to work hard to keep his voice steady. Between the frigid water and the blood pumping through his veins he felt anything but together.

"Y-your underwear is transparent." Her cheeks had turned bright red. Was that because she was embarrassed or because she couldn't control her dirty thoughts? He hoped like hell it was the latter.

# Chapter Seven

**M**J thought she'd died and gone to heaven. A heaven where the angels looked like a soaking wet Nate in very white, very transparent boxer briefs. Apparently, there were no wings or halos either. She was good with that.

"Are they?" He sounded far too innocent. But, at that moment she didn't care. What she wanted was for him to get dressed. But no, the stubborn man came over to the blanket and laid down. Stretched out within reach and let the sun kiss every inch of his skin. And she was jealous. Jealous of the sun's caress on skin she wanted to explore. Ridges and crests she wanted to trace. With her tongue.

She whimpered, and he quirked an eyebrow up in question. "Everything ok?"

"Fine." She decided to repack all the food into the basket lest she put her hands to other—far more pleasurable—tasks.

As she stacked the containers in the basket it dawned on her that she could touch him without violating her rules. A small smile escaped as she tucked the last container away. And then she turned to the half-naked man watching her with an intensity that shook her to her core.

Words were unnecessary as she scooted closer to him on her knees. She hovered over him and reached out one tentative hand. Her fingertip brushed his side and she gasped. He, on the other hand, held his breath.

He remained mute as she reached back out and made contact with his skin once more. Despite the coolness of his skin from the water, a sizzle zipped up her arm from her finger tip. She continued to trace the muscle around his rib and onto his abdomen. Where ever she touched goose-pimples broke out like a little trail.

She noticed that with each stroke of her skin against him, his cock grew harder. In turn, she grew bolder and more curious. This body of his was so different from the lean, young man's body she had once known and loved. His cock seemed somehow more, bigger. Of course that was ridiculous, but then again maybe not.

She shoved that thought aside and refocused on her exploration of his new to her physique. Up toward his pectoral muscles she continued to brush and caress as he remained utterly still for her. When she raked a nail over one pebbled nipple, he sucked in a breath and groaned.

"Babe, you're killing me."

"Is it so awful?" She imagined it was, but she wasn't quite ready to give him control. Deep inside she knew now she would give in to what she wanted, what he wanted. This whole battle to keep him away had been futile. And never had failure felt so good. Her pussy ached with desire, her nipples chafed against her sports bra, and her skin tingled with need.

She swung a leg over and straddled him, her heated center pressed against his now fully erect cock. And he grunted in response.

She unzipped her coveralls and pulled them off her shoulders. "I'm a little dirty…"

"Please, babe. Let me touch you," he rasped out.

She shook her head no. Still not done with him. Not by a long shot. She leaned over and pressed her breasts against his chest until her lips found his. With one hand on either side of his head, she traced the seam of his mouth with her tongue. Then she drove her tongue past lips and teeth to taste the man beneath her.

He moaned as his tongue wrapped around hers and then gave chase as she pulled back. But she exerted her dominance, taking control of the kiss. She licked and nibbled at his mouth until she needed to draw a real, life giving breath.

She sat back and smiled at his look of dazed desire. "Now, Nate. Touch me. Talk dirty. Get naked, now."

"Hell yeah, babe." Was all the warning she got before he had her tucked beneath him. "Now, you're mine."

He stretched her out and pressed her between his body and the ground while he pinned her arms overhead. "You and this hot, curvy little body of yours has been torturing me for ten years. And for the last week, it's been worse watching you sashay away every time you said no."

"I didn't wanna say no." She couldn't control the admission, didn't see a reason she should. "I was trying to protect myself."

He shushed her with little kisses to her sweat and dirt streaked face. "That's my job now."

That was when she realized he was kissing away her silent tears. Her heart beat slowed to match his rhythm as he wedged himself deeper between her thighs so he could press the thickness of his erection against her cleft. As he ground against her she let out the moan that had been building. The emotional turmoil of her utter surrender was lost in the dust of the awe-inspiring lust he managed to generate so quickly.

"Know what else is my job now?" He looked down at her with a wicked, sexy grin.

Stunned speechless by the raging storm inside her she shook her head in lieu of speaking.

"Your pleasure." He punctuated his statement with a circle of his hips, and she relished the friction. "I need to taste you, need to remember what it's like to have my tongue buried between your thighs."

Putting action to words, he lifted up and grabbed the bottom band of her sports bra and tugged upward until her breasts popped free of the binding material and he pulled it over her head with a little of her help. He stared at her breasts a moment, then placed a tender kiss on each puckered tip. Then he eased down her body in search of the bunched top of her coveralls. He finished unzipping them and then worked them down to her socked feet.

"Spread your legs. I want to see your pussy. See if it looks like I remember."

His voice came out rough and gravelly, which caused a shiver to ripple along her spine. He wanted her as much as she wanted him. So, she did as he requested, well demanded. Laying there, legs spread as his big hands held her thighs open, she tried not to squirm. Tried not to embarrass herself with her need. It had been over a year since her last failed attempt to find some pleasure with a man. That had been, Jack, a man she met online and dated on and off for six months. When the time had come to get naked, she couldn't get Nate out of her head. They'd gone through the motions of sex, but in the end she'd faked an orgasm just to get out of the awkward situation. Needless to say he'd never called again.

"Sweet, hell. You're soaking wet already. So sexy." Nate traced a finger along one labium and then the other. After he collected her juices on his fingertip his gaze sought hers and locked. Then he brought his finger to his mouth and sucked the glistening tip. "So sweet and tart, can't wait to lap you up."

And then he dropped to his belly and spread her lips with his thumbs as his tongue stroked her from deep between her cheeks to the sensitive bundle of nerves at the top of her slit. She jackknifed up, since his hands had pinned down her hips. "Nate!"

He grunted but continued to lick her core as he used his other hand to push her flat on the ground. He traced a little path from her hole to her clit and back again, over and over as she shot up the hill and found herself looking over the precipice of the first orgasm not delivered by her own hand in ten years.

And then he stopped.

"Oh, god. Don't stop baby." She heard the pleading in her words, but the infuriating man simply looked up at her as his mouth glistened with her wetness, and grinned. "Ten years, Nate. Ten years of only my hand. For the love of God, don't fucking stop!"

Something about her declaration caused his impossibly dark eyes to grow darker with a possessive gleam. And then he drove two fingers deep inside her as he suctioned on to her nub.

The zips and pops of pleasure cranked up a notch—or ten—and her back bowed off the ground as she tangled her fingers in his hair. He moaned against her overheated flesh and the vibrations sent her off like a roman candle. Her body soared with the pleasure firing along every nerve ending and she swore she saw a supernova. Could have just been the sun burned on to her retinas after she closed her eyes, but with the sheer bliss invading her body she didn't care to quibble.

Her sexy navy seal continued to lick and nibble at her tender pink bits until she could draw a steady breath and the aftershocks of an incredible orgasm had subsided. Sex had never been that good when they were young. No, he definitely had upped his game in the last ten years. And with that, a shadow of doubt and jealousy slithered over her joy and dampened her happiness.

Stupid, perceptive man picked up on her mood shift immediately.

He wiped his mouth with his hand and sat up. "What is it, babe?"

"Nothing." She felt stupid, childish.

"It's not nothing if it dulled the gleam of desire I worked damn hard to put on that pretty face." He reached out and cupped her cheek with his palm. "Talk to me, or this won't work no matter how explosive the sex is between us."

She sighed. "I was relishing that very fine orgasm you delivered when it dawned on me how much better at that you've gotten over the years. Which of course made me realize you probably haven't been celibate for the last decade."

He swore softly. "I won't lie to you. I haven't been a monk, but it's been a while since I last tried to be intimate with a woman. Problem was, none of them were you. So while I sought physical relief, not one of them touched my soul the way you do."

With such honest words, she knew she'd push past her pointless jealousy. He was there, with her. "I feel the same. I've tried a few time over the years, but none of them were you. In the end, I faked it every time because I wanted it to be over."

He grinned, and leaned in to kiss her. Their lips collided first, then their tongues. As passion and lust boiled over, fueled by years apart, the need to be joined together overrode all other needs.

MJ scrabbled at the waistband of his boxers and tugged. "Off."

Her one word demand between kisses was met with action. He had the damp fabric down to his knees and gone before she could make any further orders. He knelt in front of her, chest heaving with every breath, and his cock straining to the sky. He took her breath away. Without a word, he reached into the basket and pulled out a condom.

So, he came prepared. Her brow rose.

"Not a word. I told you protecting you, even from me, is my first priority. If there was even a chance you'd let me touch you I needed to be prepared. I did not assume anything." He let a slow sexy grin slide over his kiss swollen lips. "But I did hope."

She laughed. He was far too beguiling for someone as sexy as he was. She figured he'd charmed his way out of more trouble than not. And after that last coherent thought she surrendered everything to the navy seal who'd stolen her heart.

He slipped between her thighs and pressed the tip of his cock against her opening. The head stretched her as he slid in partway. Holy hell the man felt better than she remembered. Long and thick, he slowly filled her until their bodies were sealed together. Nothing about them felt wrong, especially not this part. "Love me, Nate."

"Oh babe, I never stopped." And then he slid out and shoved back in with a long easy glide that made her soul sing. Within a few strokes, she shattered around him with a loud yell that caused the birds nearby to vacate the area. He tumbled off the edge right after her and cried out his own pleasure as he strained above her balanced on his arms. He collapsed on top of her, a human blanket of flesh, muscle, and bone. Hers. "I'll always love you." His mumbled words burned through her heart as he slipped into a peaceful sleep still lodged deep in her body and soul.

# Chapter Eight

Four months later...

MJ stood in front of the mirror and checked everything one last time. It was way too cold in February for her little red sundress, but she couldn't imagine not wearing his dress when she asked Nate to marry her. She'd given him four months and with no hint of a proposal, she decided it was time to take the bull by the horns.

Also, he happened to be on leave starting on Valentine's Day. If that wasn't a sign, she didn't know what was.

The crunch of tires on the gravel drive drew her attention and had her running down the stairs to throw open the front door. Heedless of the snow and cold, she bolted out of the house wearing just her sundress and boots. Not a stitch more.

Nate was out of the truck and had his arms around her as fast as he could manage. He didn't even bother to turn off the vehicle. "You are a sight for sore eyes."

It had been a long three months since his return to duty, and she honestly hadn't expected to see him so soon, but she was damn glad about it. She was pretty sure the NSA would think she was running an internet porn site for all the hours they spent on Skype talking dirty and making it work. But now, for their first Valentine's Day in ten years, he was there. In person.

She'd started to hate the holiday, a pointed reminder of her loneliness. But, now she had Nate back in her life. He set her down, shooed her in the house to get warm, and sorted out the truck, before heading in after her. She could barely sit still as she waited for him to come in the house. Once he was inside, he hauled her into his arms and kissed her soundly. His cold hand pressed her dress against her bottom, and then flesh met flesh. He pulled away from their kiss, "A thong, babe?"

"Nope." She grinned at him.

He kissed her again, and walked them backwards until he found a wall. Then he broke the kiss, spun her around and placed her palms against the flat surface. "Don't move." He proceeded to frisk her, working his hands down her sides. He paused. "Bra?"

"Nope." She grinned and moaned as he confirmed for himself with a sweep over her hardened nipples.

Then his hands moved lower. And lower to her hips. He canted them backwards, forcing her legs back and wider than she had stood. "Stick that ass out, babe," he demanded in a low rough voice. Then he flipped the skirt of her sundress up, exposing her bare bottom. He whistled. "You know I almost brought one of my boys home with me?"

Her heart thudded in her chest. That would have been awkward. "Oh?"

"Yup. Would have been very interesting with you prancing around practically buck naked," he growled the last of his words.

"I'd have slipped inside and put on panties. Maybe." She hoped she sounded sultry and teasing.

He smacked her bare ass. "Damn right you would have. I don't share what's mine."

"Am I yours, Nate?" She needed to be reminded. Physically and emotionally. After ten years apart, she still thought she dreamed their reunion up once in a while.

"You better believe it. Need me to prove it to you?"

"Yes." She gasped as he cupped her mound from behind.

"I'd say your wet pussy should be evidence enough, babe. But maybe this will help remind you."

She heard the rustle of clothes and then his cock drove into her from behind. He grabbed her hips for leverage and fucked her hard and fast until her knees damn near gave out on her.

"See how tight you are around my cock? How perfect we fit together? Tells

148

me you're mine."

Then he reached down and rubbed over her clit until she came apart. Once the tremors eased from her body, he resumed pounding into her.

"See how fast you came for me? Tells me you're mine."

And then he broke apart behind her, shouting her name as he came.

When he pulled out of her, steadied her against the wall, and cleaned up the condom he came back with his clothes righted. She'd remained against the wall, legs trembling like a new foal.

Then he dropped to one knee.

She gasped as he pulled out a jewelry box.

"But maybe you need something like this to remind you that you're mine. That no matter the miles, no matter the time, my heart is yours and yours is mine."

She wanted to faint. She wanted to squeal. Instead she threw herself at the hulking man on his knees before her and kissed every inch of his face. In between kisses she yelled one word, over and over again. "Yes!"

The End

Thank you for reading One Night With A Cowboy! I hope you enjoyed reading these stories as much as I did writing them. If you have a moment, leaving a review would help other readers find this book, and hopefully enjoy it as much as you did. Thank you!

Of course, don't forget to sign up for my newsletter to get all the latest book news, giveaways, and other fun stuff right in your inbox!

# Other Books by Sorcha Mowbray

**Lustful Lords**

The Lustful Lords series focuses on a group of Victorian London lords who regularly gather at The Market, a notorious brothel, to indulge in hedonistic delights. As the series progresses each lord will discover a woman who is his match both in and out of the bedroom.

His Hand-Me-Down Countess (Lustful Lords, Book 1)

His Hellion Countess(Lustful Lords, Book 2)

His Scandalous Viscountess (Lustful Lords, Book 3)

His Not-So-Sweet Marchioness (Lustful Lords, Book 4)

**The Market**

*Discover the series that started it all...*

In this sizzling series The Market becomes the setting for Londoners of all walks of life to discover pleasure, lust, and even love. But can they do what is required to claim the ones they've fallen for?

Love Revealed (The Market, Book 1)

Love Redeemed (The Market, Book 2)

Love Reclaimed (The Market, Book 3)

The Market Series Books 1-3 (Boxed Set)

Love Requited (The Market, A Short Story)

# About the Author

Sorcha Mowbray is a mild mannered office worker by day…okay, so she is actually a mouthy, opinionated, take charge kind of gal who bosses everyone around; but she definitely works in an office. At night she writes romance so hot she sets the sheets on fire! Just ask her slightly singed husband.

She is a longtime lover of historical romance, having grown up reading Johanna Lindsey and Judith McNaught. Then she discovered Thea Devine and Susan Johnson. Holy cow! Heroes and heroines could do THAT? From there, things devolved into trying her hand at writing a little smexy. Needless to say, she liked it and she hopes you do too!

**You can connect with me on:**

🌐 https://sorchamowbray.com
🐦 http://twitter.com/sorchamowbray
📘 https://www.facebook.com/SorchaMowbray
🔗 https://www.instagram.com/sorchamowbray

**Subscribe to my newsletter:**

✉ https://link.sorchamowbray.com/org

.